ENVY AT THE

Lynne Bryan was born in Leicester in 1961. She now ~~~
with the writer Andrew Cowan and their daughter Rose.

Envy
at the Cheese Handout

LYNNE BRYAN

faber and faber
LONDON · BOSTON

For Andrew and Rose

First published in Great Britain in 1995
by Faber and Faber Limited
3 Queen Square London WC1N 3AU
This UK paperback edition first published in 1996

Set in Postscript Palatino by Avon Dataset Ltd, Warwickshire
Printed in England by Clays Ltd, St Ives plc

Versions of some of the stories have appeared
in the following places:

'Fish Out of Water' in *Scottish Short Stories 1994* (HarperCollins)
'A Regular Thing' in *First Fictions: Introduction 11* (Faber and Faber) and
New Writing 3 (Minerva)
'Johnny Came Courting' in *Harpies & Quines No. 7*
'Better than Beer and Skittles' in *First Fictions: Introduction 11*
(Faber and Faber) and *Original Prints Four* (Polygon)
'Family Fears' in *New Writing Scotland 11* (ASLS)
'Cat Talk' in *New Woman March 1993*
'Hair So Black' in *First Fictions: Introduction 11* (Faber and Faber)

A CIP record for this book is
available from the British Library

ISBN 0-571-17457-4

2 4 6 8 10 9 7 5 3 1

Contents

Acknowledgements

With thanks to my agent Jane Bradish-Ellames, my publishers Faber and Faber and my editor Emma Platt for their patience and support; thanks to *Harpies & Quines* and the Women's Support Project, Glasgow, for sharpening my perspective; thanks to Rose Cowan for making me laugh; and special thanks to Andrew Cowan for giving me time, encouragement and good advice.

Fish Out of Water

Monday morning Christopher phones. Christopher with his lanky body, his Roman nose. Christopher with his guilt. Ellie listens to his polite voice, the apologies which are supposed to make her feel better, the offer of money, the gift of the flat. She listens, then replaces the receiver. Quick. Before she tells him about the dark line their baby has drawn on the hump of her belly. Before she showers him with the intimacy he no longer wants. The intimacy she needs to forget.

Monday afternoon Ellie bags Christopher's belongings and leaves them on the landing outside their flat. She Hoovers the carpets, cleans every surface, empties the waste paper baskets which still hold paper scraps covered in his neat chilly writing. Then she tries to squeeze a king-size quilt into her washing machine, wanting to wash away the remnants: the smells of massage oil and sex, his naked smell. But the quilt will not fit.

Ellie will have to brave the laundrette. But it is Wednesday before she does. She has never used the laundrette, nor any of the other businesses at the end of her street. She has felt too much of an outsider, with her accent, her looks. She is not from this area.

The laundrette is crammed between the post office and the public toilets. It is an old building. Shabby. Despite the bright blue woodwork, the artfully painted sign and the Fablon fishes which swim across the display window.

The owner of the laundrette is called John. Everybody calls him John. Nobody knows his surname. The hand-painted sign above the laundrette door reads 'personal service laundrette. proprietor – john'.

John wears a deep crimson suit in winter, orange shorts in

summer. He has a lot of hats. Each day he parades the length of his laundrette, twirling like a model, showing off his clothes. The men who work at the local shipyards, with their oil-streaked skin, make a mockery of John. But others appreciate his campness, his bigger than bigness. John is their crazy man. The golden fry in their grey fry lives.

The laundrette is narrow and cluttered. Washing machines line one wall, chairs and a spin dryer the other, while at the back stands a row of ancient de luxe dryers. These dryers are buttermilk yellow, taller than a human, and look condemned. Fishes decorate most of the machines and a border of blue paint divides the concrete floor from the Artex walls.

Ellie walks to the laundrette. She feels conspicuous. Too bright for the dull buildings, the passers-by dressed in shades of brown and beige. A shabby patch. Christopher's choice because the flat was cheap and big, and besides Christopher had a car which meant he wasn't tied to the shabbiness. He could escape.

Ellie had met Christopher at work. He'd sat next to her in the canteen, causing her hands to shake nervously as she had forked her chips. She'd been flattered when he'd asked her to minute meetings for him, to move offices and cities with him, to share his life. Now, she does not know what she expected. Only she never expected his sudden resentment, his dissatisfaction. She never expected him to transfer home without her.

Ellie edges into the laundrette. She sniffs the smell of damp and standing water, registers its threadbareness, the row of customers sitting on blue plastic chairs facing the washing machines. They are local looking, sallow-skinned. But they acknowledge Ellie, make her feel welcome. Particularly the elderly women. 'Come in. Come in,' they both call.

Ellie wonders whether they are related. The way they speak together, move their heads together, heads dressed with the same short hairstyle. She notes their iron-flat bottoms and matching Crimplene trousers. One rises from her chair to transfer her washing from the washing machine to the spinner. The grey-looking garments drip on the concrete floor. The other pats the empty chair next to her, inviting Ellie to sit.

'Thank you,' says Ellie, easing on to the chair. She places her hands under her bump, lifting the weight off her bladder.

'John'll be out in a minute,' says the woman, lighting a fag. She waves it at Ellie. 'I hope you don't mind,' she says. 'But I'm terribly addicted.'

'It's OK,' says Ellie, not wishing to offend. 'I understand.'

A toilet flushes. Ellie turns towards the sound and spies a thin spout of a man. Dressed in orange shorts, scarlet shirt and green pork pie hat.

Ellie almost whistles. Like Christopher used to whistle at things strange or beautiful. An amazed whistle. A congratulatory whistle. A whistle sometimes directed at her when she wore her evening dress with the scalloped hem. The dress which made her shimmer and froth at Christopher's business meals, which she hid beneath her coat when she stepped from the flat to Christopher's car.

John sashays towards her. His hands outstretched, his face covered with ginger-red pan-stick. 'And what can I do for you?' He smiles.

Ellie holds out her bag. John up-ends it, shaking the linen on to the floor. 'Lovely,' he says. 'My speciality.'

'Oh,' says Ellie. She looks from John to her quilt. She maps the creamy stains, smells the intimate bedtime smell, and blushes. 'It's ages old,' she defends. 'I'm afraid I . . . '

John places a finger on his lips: a finger decorated with a coral ring. Shush, he mouths. Then gently he lifts the quilt to coax it in the drum of a washing machine.

'Thank you,' says Ellie, grateful for his discretion. 'Thank you very much.'

John raises his hat. 'No problem,' he says. He bends to switch on the machine, the seat of his shorts stretching to

3

frame his slim behind. Then he turns to whisper in her ear. 'If baby's pressing down,' he whispers, 'the toilet's out the back.'

'Oh,' says Ellie. 'Well it is. Yes.'

John leads Ellie to a rough tongue and groove door. The door is painted blue and has a piece of card pinned to it. The ink on the card has run and looks like a child's painting.

'Plenty of space.' John smiles as he opens the door.

Ellie manoeuvres past. She tries to return the smile, but is embarrassed, too conscious of her navel, pushed out by the developing foetus. It spoils the line of her T-shirt and threatens to finger John.

Ellie is happy to be pregnant, but also ashamed. She is ashamed of how her body has grown, how awkwardly it advertises what she wants to keep private.

She remembers having a fight with Christopher over her size. 'I'll soon be able to drown in your flesh,' he teased, pushing his face down between her breasts. A mock fight. An affectionate fight.

Ellie perches on the toilet. She runs her hands over her belly, sees the baby swim beneath her skin. Only last week she and Christopher were at the hospital, discussing his role, how he should be there when the waters break, to mop her brow, to cut the cord, to cry with her. And now?

Ellie pulls the flush, watches the greeny jet of water shoot around the dirty pan. Through the sound she can hear John, teasing his customers.

She leaves the toilet to find him seated at a tatty card table. The table is piled with mail, a silver-coloured cash box and a newspaper. The newspaper is folded, with the quick crossword showing. John lifts a pen from a small leather pouch strung around his waist and taps it on the crossword.

The woman with the fag invites Ellie to sit again. She leans towards Ellie, cigarette ash dressing her chin. 'This is fun,' she confides.

4

'Now . . . ' says John. He stretches his arms, links his fingers together, pushing till they crack. 'What's got eight letters, begins with S and means to pl . . . unge?' John dips his hands deep beneath the table.

'Or to s . . . ink?' John nips his nose between his fingers, makes glug glug noises like an emptying drain.

A man nearing eighty shuffles to look at the crossword. He wears a full three piece suit and a kipper tie. He has no teeth and seems unable to form proper words. John winks at him. 'Not you Joe,' he says. 'You concentrate on your smalls. I'm wanting an answer from the smart girls. Margaret? Mary?'

The two elderly women shake their heads. 'No idea, John,' they say.

'How about you, then?' asks John, looking at a boy.

The boy lowers his eyes, moves to watch his football kit and track pants flick their desultory way around the innards of a de luxe dryer. The dryer slows and the boy clicks open the door to pull out the load. John walks over to help him. He takes the washing from the boy's arms and stuffs it in a bin bag. 'Submerge,' he says to the boy. 'The word I'm looking for is submerge. I submerge. You submerge. We all submerge.'

The boy says, 'Oh.' He slips a hand into his trouser pocket, removes some change. John watches the boy as he fumbles to select the right coins.

'Here, let me,' John says. He takes the boy's hand, spreading the slight palm flat with his ringed fingers. 'Just like choosing chocolates,' he winks. He lifts the coins. One by one. Fake kissing the queen's head before dropping them, chinking, into his leather pouch.

'Don't be wicked, John,' laughs the elderly woman with the fag. 'You'll embarrass the boy.' Smoke rushes from her mouth and Ellie shifts heavily in her chair, turning her head from the smell.

John ushers the boy from the laundrette, then wanders over to look at Ellie's washer. 'The red light is out,' he says. Ellie grips the plastic chair and tries to push herself up. 'No, don't.'

John flags her to sit. 'I'll put it in the dryer. We can't have you straining yourself.'

John pulls the quilt from the washer. Ellie notices that the quilt is not whiter than white, that some stains remain. John lifts the quilt, holds it to the light. 'Not bad,' he comments. 'Not as bad as old Mac's. Remember that, ladies? He swore it was just dirt. I told him just dirt wouldn't stick to the fabric like that. Just dirt would disappear.' John bundles the quilt in a de luxe dryer and slams shut the glass dome door.

'Ah, but he's a weird one,' remarks the elderly woman with the fag. She moves the fag like she is underlining words on a blackboard, a teacher making a point.

Ellie closes her eyes and bathes in the sound of John and his customers. She's been alone since Christopher left, more so since his call. Her only company has been the television, and the muffled voices of her neighbours. The muffled angry voices which seep through the thin wall behind her bookcase, which belong to the young couple who ignore her, who ran coins down the side of Christopher's car.

The woman with the clothes in the spinner removes them. She holds each item against her face to test for dampness, before stuffing it in her basket on wheels. 'Well,' she says. 'That's me.'

'And that's £2.50,' says John.

The woman nods and opens her plastic purse. She fumbles around. 'More bus tickets than money,' she sighs.

The elderly man laughs. 'Shut it you,' says John. 'Or you're banned.'

'Don't ban,' begs the elderly man. 'Don't ban.' He looks down at his kipper tie, touches its flowery point.

'Bless him,' says the woman with the fag.

'Oh, don't be conned,' says John. He places an arm round the elderly man's shoulders. The man smiles at John and makes loving noises. 'This guy is fly. He gets tea and biscuits from me every day, and not once has he paid for his washing.'

'Perhaps I should play potty,' says the woman. 'Get my stuff done for free.'

'And do me out of business?' John winks. 'You'd miss me, Mary. I'm the only man in your life.'

'Some man,' laughs the woman. She edges towards John, puckering her lips.

Ellie is the last to leave the laundrette. Her quilt has taken a long while to dry in the de luxe dryer. John apologizes, but she says it doesn't matter, that she has enjoyed her morning. 'I was feeling a little sad,' she says. 'You've cheered me up.'

'Glad to hear it,' smiles John. 'I do my best.' He gestures at the machinery, now standing idle on the bare concrete floor, the plastic measuring cups empty of soap powder, the tatty price list peeling from the wall. 'It's difficult, but . . . ' He smiles again.

'Yes,' says Ellie. 'It is.' She pays John, and carries her quilt from the laundrette. John bolts the laundrette door behind her, turning his OPEN sign to WE ALL NEED LUNCH BREAKS.

Alone on the street Ellie feels a chill. A cool breeze carrying the stench of the nearby sewerage works, the sounds of mothers chastising their kids, those distinctive guttural voices that Christopher used to mimic. Ellie glances back to the warmth of the laundrette, wanting to quell the rush of memories, the bleakness she almost forgot while guessing crossword clues, watching John parade his costume, tilting his pork pie at enticing angles.

She returns to squint through the murky glass, hoping to reassure herself. A last glimpse of someone as alien as her. Yet managing. Like a fish out of water. Turned amphibious.

When Ellie arrives at her flat she unbundles her quilt, lays it on the bed. She smells the sweet smell of cheap soap powder, traces the mottled pattern of diminished stains. She climbs beneath the quilt, piles pillows under her belly and curls to rest.

7

She closes her eyes, and recalls John as she saw him through the laundrette window. He was leaning into a de luxe dryer, wiping a rag around the drum. A dull shift pulled over his bright bright clothes. A shift which he hadn't worn when surrounded by customers. A shift which made her shiver and fear for herself. Until John turned round to acknowledge her tapping upon the pane. His smile golden, joyous, unchanged.

At least that was how Ellie saw the smile. Needing to ignore the brief moment before when John had looked different. His face as chilly and grey as the concrete floor of his laundrette. His slight form swamped by the ageing machinery, mocked by the flicking tails of his Fablon fishes.

A Regular Thing

I'm confused. For years I hoped Emily would stop charging me. Now she has I find I don't want it. I feel the bottom has dropped out of my life. I feel threatened, insecure.

I'm thirty-six. I first met Emily when I was twenty-nine. At Astley Central Library.

I started work in the library at sixteen. A natural step: I've always been fond of books and during school days was nick-named SS (Studious Steven). But I'm not intellectual. Most books are beyond me. Like the books Emily reads on advanced economics.

I'm just comforted by books. Well-thumbed books with cheesy pages and broken spines. Like the paperbacks in the Romance section. At sixteen I kept away from Romance, thought it sissy. Now I'm Section Head.

I met Emily two months into my promotion. I was rummaging behind the loans counter for the most recent edition of the *Romance Writers' Quarterly* when I heard coughing. The coughing was accompanied by a voice. Such a voice, husky but efficient. 'Excuse me,' it said. 'But I'm in a rush. Can you stamp my books now?'

Used to disappointments I expected the voice to belong to an elderly spinster with a smoker's larynx. So I was abrupt. 'Sorry,' I said. 'I don't work the loans counter. I'll get Miss Pedi to deal with you. Miss Pedi!'

Then I saw Emily. My eyes worked upwards from her girlie breasts to her face with its cold eyes, its bob of oily hair. My heart somersaulted and my penis began to stiffen. I rubbed it casually against the loans counter.

9

'Hello,' said Emily. 'I'm called Emily.'

'Steven,' I replied.

'Steven,' she said. 'Nice name. Before Miss Pedi comes can I ask a question?'

I nodded, flushed. Something told me the question wouldn't be about books.

I'm not usually daring. I tend to stand back, watch others walk into the lions' den. But Emily bewitched me. She has tremendous power. She knows how to make a coward brave.

When we met at the fountain she looked like a lonely man's dream: tight black jumper, skirt and those little lace-up booties with pointy heels made from shiny plastic. I felt ill-equipped. 'I haven't much money,' I said. I clutched my thin wallet; even as Section Head I earn less than my father who sweeps for Astley Precision Tools. 'I can stretch to a Chinese and a couple of beers.'

Emily smiled, an amazing smile, lips curling back to show their fleshy pink underside. 'What do we want with a Chinese?' she said. 'Let's make our own entertainment.'

Emily took me to her home, a flat above a baby wear shop. A small flat with one main room painted white. Two archways led from this room. Through one archway was a kitchen; through the other, the bathroom. Swinging bead curtains hung from each archway. They were identical, depicting a cinema usherette wearing a skimpy pink bunny outfit. Around the usherette's neck hung a tray. The tray rested on her large breasts. She smiled a big smile, and a bubble led from the smile. 'Peanuts, sir?' she asked.

I didn't know what to make of the flat. It was so sparse. The bead curtains provided the only real decoration and they seemed deliberately over the top. Like they'd been chosen as a statement. But I couldn't work out the statement. They hung there, shimmering, threatening. And instead of asking Emily about them, I turned to her bookcase.

The bookcase ran between the curtains. It was huge. Filled

with books. For a while, I examined the books. They were all on finance. 'What's wrong, Steven?' asked Emily. She slid a thin arm round my shoulders.

'There's not a novel in sight,' I said.

'Or a book about women's troubles.' She laughed. 'I'm a practical girl. I'm into what makes the world go round.'

'Money,' I said.

'And sex.' She took my hand and led me to the only other piece of furniture in the room – her bed.

I'd dated before Emily. Mostly nice girls with soft bodies and big eyes. Willing girls. But unadventurous. No costumes. No games. No dirty talk. No slapping, kicking, punching or spitting. Emily sat astride me, bending her arms behind her back, making her small breasts point forward like individual jellies, and showed me what I'd been missing. She made me feel like a king, a conqueror. 'Emily,' I said. 'That was wonderful.'

Afterwards I thought we'd have a drink, swap stories, relax with each other, feel our way. But no. She started talking business. 'That one was for free,' she said. 'Charging first time is always counter-productive. You'll not come back for more. Not unless you're desperate. And I don't want you if you're desperate.'

I don't consider myself an idiot. But perhaps I am. Perhaps Emily saw me coming. Sometimes I check myself in the mirror, to see if it's written over my face. But there are no clues. Only my spectacles, my thin mouth, my blondish hair, my bad skin stare back.

'But Emily,' I protested. She placed a finger on my lips and hushed me.

'Don't knock it,' she said. 'It's a good deal.'

My body was hungry for Emily so I began to see her on a regular basis, once a week, twenty pounds a time. But I wasn't swept along. Mentally I kept distant, tried to sort out the situation. I took to spying on her.

Early mornings, library lunchtimes, dinnertimes and most evenings I waited outside her flat to catch her at it. But no men in dirty rainmacs, no young boys anxious to lose their virginity, only a small woman dressed in a suit and carrying a briefcase.

'So Emily, you're not a prostitute?' I asked, casually as I could. She lay on her bed, looking wonderful: her top half naked, her legs covered with a wrap of black silk.

'No,' she said in her husky voice. 'I'm your lover.'

'But then why do you charge me?'

Emily explained. She said men had treated her badly. They had taken her love and used it against her. So now she charged. Because charging meant she was in control, charging meant she was safe. She spoke matter of factly, like she was reading a shopping list. But I believed her. It made sense to me.

The confidence strengthened our relationship. We began to see more of each other, took the test and stopped using condoms, and though Emily continued to ask for money I felt encouraged, hopeful. I imagined a day when we'd be like any normal couple, exchanging our love freely.

After a year we bought a flat together and I took Emily to meet my parents. They hated her. On sight. They wouldn't admit to it. They were polite. They asked her about her job, gave her ham and salad sandwiches, iced fancies and a cup of weak tea. But you could see it in their eyes. My mother looked Emily up and down. As she took in Emily's thigh boots, hot pants and Lycra top, her face was blank, her pupils marked with distaste. She actually said, 'A word in your ear, Steven. Is this the right kind of girl for you? Isn't she a bit unclean?'

I replied, 'I love her, Mother. We get on well together.'

Then I began to feel less positive. There were days when I'd look at our relationship and see nothing. Emily and I would meet after work, go out for a meal or to the pictures, return home and yet still seem separate. I knew it wasn't my fault. I offered myself; told her my history, my likes and dislikes, my longings. But Emily was so closed, only gave out at night when we touched. And she spoilt that by charging.

At one point I nearly cracked. Her charges rose above the rate of inflation. They began to cripple me. And I had to take an extra job, collecting pools monies from Astley's nastiest estate – Craigheath. It wasn't a pleasant job. I had a couple of dangerous customers who once got me in a back alley. They beat me. They took off my glasses, stood me against a wall and pushed ring-covered hands into my face. 'Poor poor Steven,' cooed Emily when I returned home.

'You could stop it, you know,' I said to her as she dabbed a cotton wool ball over my cheeks, nose, ears. The ball was soaked in Dettol. It stung. To take my mind off the pain I concentrated on Emily's breasts which moved across my chest, tickling.

'How can I stop it?' she asked, innocent. 'Should I take up karate, go out for revenge?'

I squeezed her hand. The Dettol trickled brown down her skinny wrist. 'Getting ready to thump me now, are you?' she said. Her eyes were strangely bright.

I went to the doctor. I told Emily it was because my wounds were infected. It wasn't a total untruth. Blue-green pus lined a cut which ran across my cheek.

I chose a locum. I didn't want to confess to my regular, who'd seen me grow, who'd watched my testicles drop. The locum traced her gentle finger along the cut, then asked me what I'd really come for. 'Sexual problems?' she asked.

'Sort of,' I confided.

The locum listened carefully. She nodded her head, made notes. 'I think you should approach the mother,' she advised. 'You shouldn't blame the mother, mothers get blamed for too many things. But I think you should have a chat. Mothers can be very helpful.'

Emily's mother dresses like a man. She favours double-breasted suits made from merino. Beneath which she wears a white shirt and a yellow or black tie. She sports cufflinks, Argyle socks and brogues. Her hair is cut to the scalp; her face free of make-up.

Emily introduced us at the flat-warming. I recognized her immediately. 'You used to visit Emily at her old place,' I said. 'Tuesdays and Thursdays. I saw you.'

'Yes,' said Emily's mother. 'I know all about your spying.'

I hated her then. Now not at all. She speaks her mind and, beneath the macho stuff, has a heart. Emily loves her too. The flat seems to lighten when she's around. There's more laughter, and Emily opens up, tells stories I've never heard before.

It took me a while to confide in Emily's mother. I was reticent because I thought she didn't like men. I imagined her as a woman's woman. Of course I couldn't ignore the evidence. But somehow I thought of Emily as a one-night stand: Emily's mother lying back and taking it because she wanted a child. But no.

Emily's mother is hetero through and through. 'She's a real fire-cracker,' my boss, Mr Brudly, disclosed. 'A rare and dangerous woman. Our affair lasted five months.'

'Yes,' said Emily's mother when I faced her. 'It ended badly. I told him it was over whilst waiting my turn at the Outpatients.'

Then I learnt that Emily's mother knew about her daughter. About how she charged me. 'Emily has told me all,' she said. 'But there's little I can do. My daughter's headstrong, opinionated. She'll always approach life her own way. You could try to make her jealous. But that's a crude device. I suggest if you love her, then just persevere.'

'But,' I said, lifting my head from her fly-buttoned lap. 'But I don't even know if she cares for me. She's so controlled.'

Six months ago, Emily made the spare room into an office. She

14

left her job as financial advisor for Dryson, Dryson and Sons to go it alone. I was worried. For a while I thought it'd cost me more for sex. Extra revenue to cover loss of earnings, or to fund the computer, desk, headed notepaper, filing cabinets, photocopier and electronic pencil sharpener. But she didn't seem to need it. Emily poached clients from her old firm. She ran an advertising campaign which promised personal service; a promise headlining beneath a profile shot of Emily looking her best. Soon her desk diary was full and she was having to turn away clients.

She now has a host of regulars. Mostly men, though some are women. The women power-dress and carry briefcases. They snub me. The men wink.

I was jealous of the men. I took a fortnight off work to check Emily was giving them financial advice and nothing else. One evening she came to me and said, 'This business is kosher, Steven. I only want to sleep with you.'

That night Emily and I had our first real row. From opposite sides of the bedroom we slung insults, grievances. Emily said I was a typical chauvinist. I told her she was a typical whore. We made our demands: Emily wanting to be loved for herself, me wanting free sex.

That argument may have been behind Emily's change of mind. That and my decision to become celibate. Though I still desired her, I turned my back on her.

Eventually she confronted me, complained that her incomings from our sex were at an all time low. 'Why, Steven?' she asked.

She looked confused when I explained. 'This isn't normal, Emily,' I said. 'My paying you has to stop. It puts a barrier between us. I've lived with you for years and still don't know what you're thinking. Since meeting you I've been on an emotional roller-coaster. I'm tired out.'

She watched me closely. Her cold blue eyes unsympathetic, searching. I began to cry. I lifted my hand to my face, and that was when she changed. The eyes stayed the same cold blue, but her chin, her cheeks, her mouth lost their hard edge. She wasn't my Emily.

A week later she handed me a letter to read on my way to work. I slid it in my jacket pocket, fearful of the white envelope, the bold 'STEVEN' on the front.

I entered Elder Park, found a bench by the pond. The sun shone, gardeners raked stray twigs and Coke cans from the murky water, the boat-keeper untied the paddle boats. I listened to the sound of rope dragging across wood. Then I opened the letter.

At first I couldn't read the writing. It seemed to blur, and inside I felt sick, imagined Emily was saying goodbye. When I could focus I was surprised to see her words stretched across the page, gigantic, urgent, saying something very different.

'Dear Steven, I've decided to stop charging you. It doesn't make sense. We've been together for so long. Let's start afresh. Emily.'

I read the letter three times. Each time I felt more elated, felt my future advancing – hopeful, warm, blessed.

Now I'm not so sure.

Emily hasn't charged me for a while. In the early days it was glorious. Real pleasure. I found my wallet growing fat. I treated myself to new clothes, bought Emily finance books and sexy underwear. We made love whenever and wherever. The foreplay was exploratory. Our caresses not governed by how much I could afford. And after sex we would open up, reveal our fears, desires. Emily had some terrible tales to tell. A man had once tried to set fire to her, threw a lighted box of matches at her hair. Another man had kept her locked in his room, chained to his bed. I would hug her as she spoke of these things. And she was generous. When I spoke of my past and my petty difficulties with girls who'd behaved too nicely, she never condemned, never claimed her experiences as more

16

important, more painful. Then she flipped.

I should've seen it coming. Emily is a professional. If she chooses to do something she does it right. She does not cut corners. She began to borrow books from my section of the library. She would devour the slim pink volumes, jot down endless notes on Romance. She would take these notes everywhere with her, consult them when washing, eating.

She wears rose print dresses now. Puts a large silk ribbon in her hair to soften it. She's talking of selling her business. She wants me to be the breadwinner, while she stays at home. She wants to get married. She wants to have children. She's become submissive, her conversation punctuated with phrases like 'Whatever you think, darling', her lovemaking conventional. She's lost her cold cold gaze.

Last night, I telephoned her mother. 'Please do something,' I begged. 'I can't stand this. It's torture.'

Emily's mother laughed. 'I've told you before, Steven, I have no control over my daughter. She's stubborn. Besides, why are you complaining? Isn't she giving you what you've always wanted?'

I was silent.

'Well, isn't she?' pushed Emily's mother.

'I suppose,' I replied. 'I really don't know.'

This morning I wake, raise myself on an elbow, watch Emily as she sleeps. She is very beautiful. Despite the little girl ribbon. Despite the flannelette nightie. I touch her upon the shoulder, brush a hair from her mouth.

I am so confused. I wonder whether I should've let things be, not forced her to change. I have no answer. I feel like the floor has been taken from under me. That I have nothing solid to stand on. I feel desperate.

Cave Dreams

The cave is larger than Pat remembers, and colder, much colder. She drops her rucksack and stands for a while looking at her new home.

The afternoon light flows through the enormous mouth, illuminating the space inside. Pat searches for the sheltered dip at the back where she slept with Judith and there it is. No mistaking. The floor, the carpet of earth, is visible and recognizable too. But the rest seems different, very different.

The walls are more curvaceous, billowing out like cheeks puffed with air. Solid cheeks, damp cheeks made from a stone shiny with a sprinkling of silver on grey, gashes of rusty red and blue and green. The roof is rounded also, not a smooth round, but pitted and funnelled like the fleshy skin of some internal organ.

Pat opens her rucksack, empties her clothes and sleeping bag on the cave floor. She then goes outside for her other materials. She has five boxes packed with batteries and matches, candles and torches, distress flares, juice and water, dried fruit and pulses, crockery and cutlery, DIY tools, a Primus, seeds and bulbs, polythene, books, writing and drawing materials. She also has a large plastic dustbin which she intends to use to store her foodstuffs and anything else which may need to be kept from the wet and damp.

Pat has only just emptied her boxes, snacked and laid out her sleeping bag when the night surprises her. Its dark comes suddenly, bitterly. She strikes a few matches, but the tiny flames barely penetrate. She needs a torch and candles, but can't find them in the mess which surrounds her. She hasn't had time to unwrap all her possessions, to find a proper place for them inside her cave. She feels a few packages, but is unable to distinguish the shapes.

She gives up to snuggle inside her sleeping bag. She tries to sleep, but it is too silent, too still. It isn't the same as the night she curled up with Judith. Her friend's snores made the surroundings seem homely. Now, Pat has only the monotonous roll of the sea, and occasionally an animal or bird noise, and from further away sounds like cracking wood.

Pat knows the date and place of her birth, but not the name of her mother and father. She grew up in care. Until she had her own daughter she never considered her background, her upbringing. It was just there. It was her. It was like a colour she carried around inside her; an institutional beige which barely warmed her blood.

Her daughter was six months old when Pat realized she'd been cheated. Melissa was lying on her back on her changing mat and Pat was cleaning her bottom, when she suddenly looked up to smile a proper smile. It was a beautiful gummy grin and it made Pat weep.

It came to Pat then that she didn't know who'd witnessed her first smile, which member of staff, which paid parent. A flood of images followed of narrow corridors filled with wandering children, of beds and tables and chairs, mealtimes in a barn-like hall, chats and cuddles cut short when a shift came to its end.

The memories angered her, made her resentful. She took it out on Melissa. She was jealous of what her daughter had – a mother, a father, a home. And it was worse in the summer. The sun shone, and it opened Pat out. She'd ache with good humour and she'd forget herself. She'd sing and dance and would spin Melissa round in her arms. Then as Melissa began to giggle, as she began to enjoy herself, Pat would suddenly remember. She'd stop, put Melissa on the ground, stand over her and watch her cry for more.

It takes Pat months to settle, to get used to new sleeping and waking times, the loneliness, the vagaries of the weather, the strange inhuman sounds.

At the start she wants to go with nature, to fit in with its demands. She doesn't want to intrude, to alter her environment to make

19

life more comfortable, though she has the tools and equipment to do so. She shivers in her sleeping bag, endures the condensation, lets the mouth of the cave suck in the wind to chill her and scatter her bits and pieces.

By April she is already weak. Her back aches, her arms and legs ache. Her hair falls out as she combs it. She realizes she'll have to do something. She'll have to domesticate to survive.

She battles to collect driftwood, to make a windbreak inside the cave, and behind the break a small shelter like a wooden tent. She covers the sloping walls of the shelter with polythene and digs a trench at the base of the walls to catch the condensation. She makes a platform inside the shelter to sleep on.

She clears a narrow path to the pool of fresh water which sits at the top of the cliff. She creates a garden of raised beds outside the cave and fills it with earth from the far end of the beach. She plants herbs, cabbage, carrots and lettuce in the rich soil.

By June the sun is beginning to shine and Pat feels more in control. She is aware of what she needs to do in order to live and she arranges her days accordingly. She has an eating, sleeping, cleaning, gardening and scavenging routine. As she becomes expert at her tasks the days seem to loosen and lengthen. She finds she has spare time, and uses it to reflect.

Pat told no one of her feelings. There was no one to tell. Melissa's father was kind enough, but he avoided conversation. He preferred the television. He liked horses and football, dog racing and darts. He wanted his world to be easy and simple and empty, and for Pat to get on with hers. He became muddled when she left him. He'd never imagined anything was wrong.

Pat joined a single mothers' group and spent Wednesday afternoons unburdening herself. Melissa would be doing PE at school and Pat would be trying to unravel the bitterness which had knotted her heart.

Pat met Judith at the group, and she became Pat's best and closest friend. Judith is a well-meaning woman, who now struggles with her conscience, blaming herself for Pat's strange behaviour, the illness which made Pat want to leave her daughter, her job, leave everything to live in a cave.

The summer is glorious. The days are longer. The sky bluer. The wind less wild and bitter. Pat's garden flourishes, she flourishes.

Often she goes about her chores completely naked, feeling skittish and carefree, relishing the sun on her limbs, the open air tingling her skin. She dances crazy jigs in the mouth of her cave, makes patterns on the beach with seaweed and shells. She spends as long as possible outside and at the close of these days she falls effortlessly into a blissful sleep, her dreams filled with frolicking fish and the lulling sound of a calm, beatific sea.

Judith works as a school dinner-lady, but she isn't excited by bangers and mash, orange jellies set with satsumas and topped with cold custard. She would prefer to be a counsellor.

She saw the ad for the night class in the local freesheet and Pat encouraged her to enrol. Judith is a sympathetic listener, unafraid of giving advice, but not out to control. She was accepted on to the course without any trouble and became enthused as Pat knew she would.

Judith showed Pat her book lists, her photocopied handouts. Pat scanned the titles, stumbled over the difficult words. She was impressed, more so when she read Judith's essays, the tutor's encouraging comments scrawled in the margins.

Judith's tutor was attracted to theories about the inner child. Judith repeated her lectures to Pat. Pat understood little, but she felt a buzzing in her friend and over the weeks she became convinced that Judith was on to something, something which could help.

For Pat needed help – she wasn't right, and her mind was the problem. Lately it had begun to confuse her, it would feel muggy but there'd be something working busily in there, something Pat couldn't reach, something unformulated, fluid and vast. And worse, her nights were punctuated by terrible dreams; loosely woven dreams crammed with women – old women, young women, girl babies, families of females. They all looked very familiar, but Pat couldn't name or place them. Their talk was loquacious, their laughter chilling. Pat would wake feeling possessed, occupied by lives more substantial than her own, threateningly solid.

Judith felt too much of a novice to give Pat the help she wanted, too inexperienced to counsel. And she thought it would spoil their friendship. She told Pat to contact a professional. But Pat didn't want a stranger; she wanted Judith, her sympathetic pal. She pleaded and pleaded; Judith wasn't strong enough to resist.

'So what would you like to talk about?' Judith asked in Pat's living room. Judith was perched on a high-backed wooden chair, she rested a clipboard and a box of tissues on her lap. Pat lay on the sofa.

'I don't know,' replied Pat. She was nervous. She closed her eyes, tried to think how to begin.

Judith leant forward, her large breasts drooping to rest on the tissue box, and she smiled. 'Come on Pat, don't be afraid.'

The summer is glorious, but cannot be trusted. The rain arrives suddenly, drives Pat to her cave. She tries to occupy herself with tidying the place, cooking a meal, reading a book, but it doesn't prevent the thoughts from cluttering in. Her sunny mind becomes heavy, a pain tightens behind her eyes and, because there is no Judith to talk to, she takes up her hand mirror and stares at her reflection.

Pat's appearance is troubling her. It is no longer youthful; her neck sags, her mouth is thinning and lines pucker the skin below her nose. Her face is aging and she cannot predict what will transpire. She doesn't know her ancestors. She has no pictures of elderly parents or other relatives to compare herself with. She has no clues as to how her nose will look when really old, or her forehead, or her ears. She does not know if she will get liver spots, gain weight or lose it.

She lies down with the mirror clasped to her chest and her eventual sleep is fitful and scary. She has a dream, it comes to her most evenings. The cave is an enormous womb and Pat is knocking around inside it, forty-five years old, but stripped and bald and curled like a foetus. A gale blows, lifting Pat's mature and embryonic self, gusting her, battering her against the pulsating cave walls which look like flesh and blood, which are coloured like membrane, but which bruise and cut her like rock.

Pat went to pieces soon after her first session with Judith. She couldn't sleep, couldn't eat, couldn't wash or dress. She let mould grow inside her waste paper baskets. She forgot to water her house plants and was unmoved when their leaves crisped, dropped off to die. She lounged on her sofa, staring at the television, hopping channels with the remote control. Her body felt weak, her mind hyperactive – it buzzed with incomprehensible images, flickerings of colour and fuzzy white squiggles.

Judith referred to her course books, her notes, her tutor's teachings. She role-played with her reflection. But she found no solutions, nothing to heal Pat's terrible anguish. Judith called the doctor. He spent five minutes with Pat and diagnosed nervous debility. He wrote her a line.

'Your friend needs a holiday,' the doctor confided to Judith. 'She's a little overwrought.'

Judith sniffed wetly. 'I think it's my fault.'

The doctor took Judith's hands, pressed them and said, 'Don't blame yourself. Your friend is just one of these ladies; she's a fragile flower, too delicate for life.'

Judith pursued the doctor as he edged out to his Audi. 'But a holiday may help?'

'A holiday,' confirmed the doctor. 'Plenty of fresh air and no navel gazing.'

And so Judith frantically arranged a weekend break. She phoned a women's charity to beg for money. She described her and Pat's penurious circumstances, Pat's ill health, how they both needed to get away. She swore her allegiance to the feminist cause and received enough cash to fund their fares.

But Pat didn't want to go. She was too frightened to shift. Her head felt hot, combustible, and she believed any activity would set it alight. Judith pleaded. She showed Pat photographs of their destination, their train and ferry tickets, the nylon rucksacks she'd bought from Camping Crazy in the indoor market. She implored, she cajoled. But it was Melissa, Pat's daughter, who finally got Pat to move.

The young woman entered the living room and stood before her mother. She wore a loose beaded smock, her hair hung in braids. 'Mum,' she said. 'You've got to get well. You have responsibilities. I'm pregnant.'

The summer turns and Pat sits in the mouth of her cave. Her long grey hair is bundled high on her head. It is dotted with sea mist and sparkles when caught by the weakening sun. Her face is naked and leathery. She is dressed in layers of tatty jumpers and T-shirts and leggings. She wears scuffed mountain boots without laces. She hugs her knees, draws them closer to her chest, and she sleeps as she sits.

Pat dreams she is fresh to the world, less than a year old. She sees herself in a flouncy dress, white socks and patent shoes. She is trying to pull herself up to take her first steps. She has her hands on the leg of a painted wooden chair. Someone is watching her efforts. A woman across the room from her. She can see the woman's grey pumps, the hem of her pink staff uniform. But the woman doesn't speak to Pat to encourage her, and she doesn't help Pat when she falls.

'Judith!' Pat cries as she falls. She falls through the floor to a world strewn with rocks, jagged rocks poking high into the sky like serrated shark fins. Pat feels their nasty edges cut into her, shredding her skin, snagging her bones. And it is almost a relief when the sea pushes in, pushes over the brutal land to claim her, to sweep her away.

The weather was fine, a cool breeze, a bright turquoise sky. The ferry barely rocked as it inched from the mainland harbour across the waters to the small isle. Judith stood on deck, her arms encircling her friend. 'Are you OK?' she asked Pat.

Pat nodded, though she wasn't sure. Her body was stronger, her mind less busy, but still she felt diminished. And Judith wasn't helping. She fussed around Pat, eyeing her close for signs of dementia. 'Relax,' said Pat.

Things improved after they disembarked. The holiday seemed to take them over, to shift their focus outwards. They checked in at the island's only hotel and walked into the wilds. They found abandoned crofts, standing stones, hills and stretches of land covered with coarse grass and patches of flowers.

When they reached the coast again, they clambered along a rugged cliff top and looked down to see a bay dotted with black and yellow seaweed and boulders, and later a beautiful broad sweep of a beach, a perfect beach, flat and glistening and coloured a cool gold, like the white gold of a wedding ring.

They sat and watched the wide bleak ocean meet the precious sands. They spied the shiny nubbed heads of seals poking through the sea's skin. They watched seagulls and guillemots swoop across the greying sky. Until it began to rain, serious rain, heavy ceaseless unapologetic rain.

They put on their waterproofs and thought about returning to the hotel, but knew they'd never make it. The blanket of rain obscured the route back.

'Shelter,' Judith shouted. 'We need shelter.' Her voice was muffled, rain poured from the tip of her nose like water from a jug. She found the way down, edging from rock to rock, and Pat followed, carefully, trying not to slip.

Pat saw the cave first, its enormous mouth which appeared as vast and black as the entrance to their city's underpass. But not as timid, not dressed with lights and road lanes and metal crash barriers. A real dark gaping hole.

She pointed it out to Judith and they struggled towards it, the rain weighting their clothes, the sand sucking at their boots.

The cave was nice inside, it felt warm. Its wide mouth nar-

25

rowed to form a snug space at the back where the floor was soft and yielding. It was comfortable.

The friends settled themselves. They opened their packed lunches and ate whilst watching the downpour. And when the sky turned from rain black to dusky gloom they decided to spend the night there. They huddled together, and soon Judith began snoring her usual rapid snore and Pat slipped into a heavy dreamless sleep, the soundest sleep, the best she'd had for weeks.

In the morning Pat woke early, stepped from the cave to view the sun rise over the sea. The air was cool. It smelt fresh, enlivening. She checked how far the waves had travelled up the beach overnight, reassured herself they could never reach as far as the cave. Then she walked the sands.

When she told Judith about her idea her friend nodded, bemused. She was barely awake and in her drowsy state forgot Pat was sick. 'Oh yes?' Judith smiled. 'Oh yes? You'll get piles.'

She brushed her hand through her short thick hair, then along a ledge in the cave, where the previous night's condensation had gathered. 'And rheumatism.' She laughed.

The weeks pass, the weather turns very cold, the air clammy, perpetually damp. Huddling in her cave, Pat boils some water on her small Primus, makes a pot of tea and a bowl of noodles.

She crawls into her bed place with her food, trying to keep herself warm. The condensation makes its steady drip drip on to the sloped walls of the shelter. Pat pulls her sleeping bag over her legs, wishing the sound would go away. It is hypnotic, it mixes and merges with the soft swooshing of the sea outside. It lulls.

Pat feels herself drifting, her head getting heavy. Another noise pulses in the background. It pulses louder and Pat tries to locate it, sensing it is man-made, from somewhere other than here. It sits intrusively in her mind, the soft steady hum of the monitoring machine.

And in the labour suite Pat looks on as the baby splits Melissa, breaks from her with such force that blood and tissue shower the nurses, splattering their candy-striped uniforms and white paper hats. The cord is cut and Pat is handed her new granddaughter, a squelchy, repulsive bundle. Pat baulks at the infant, throws her in the air as she flees from the room.

Pat does not deserve this. She is so very tired. She wants sleep, but does not want this kind which pulls her about, exhausts and frightens her. She shivers, and the motion tips her noodles into her lap. Wearily she scoops up the soggy pile , opens her shelter door, and discards the mess. There is daylight outside, it is still afternoon.

Pat climbs the rugged path which winds from the beach to the cliff top. Sharp shingle and pebbles dig into the soles of her boots. A drizzly wind wets her face and neck and bare hands. She continues on for a mile, descending then rising again, following the curve of her bay, further than she has ventured before. She treads a flat field of mud and coarse grass, clambers a plain of stones and boulders, out to a rocky promontory. The wind gusts fiercely, blows her hair in her eyes. She pulls away the sticky strands and stares at the view before her.

There is water all around her and Pat can see another side to the island, a very different shoreline to the sands of her own. Pat finds it hard to believe they belong to the same isle: her glistening sands and this gloomy and miserable coast. Here are the rocks of her dreams, serrated and jagged.

She descends towards them as early evening closes in.

Judith and Pat got drunk before Pat set out for the island. They sat in Pat's front room and downed gin and sherry and lager and even the odd glass of cherry liqueur which Pat's husband had given her after their split.

Pat lay down, snuggled her head on Judith's belly. She listened to her friend's innards as they worked, swallowing the drink, churning it, slooshing it round and down, and she heard Judith's voice sounding far away, strange, as Judith broached the subject which now rattled them both.

'You needn't go,' Judith said. 'This is foolish. It's not going to make you better, and Melissa needs you.'

Pat kept her head on Judith's ample stomach. She couldn't reply, felt unable to tell Judith that Melissa was making it worse, that she couldn't stand her daughter's new shape, the bulge which was beginning to show.

She shivered, and Judith said carefully, thoughtfully, 'Birth always prompts painful memories. It's natural. It makes you think about your babyhood, your baby's babyhood, childhood, families, the life continuum which goes on regardless of past damage, hurt, pain. Here's another baby, but nothing is healed, you're not healed.'

'I don't need this,' Pat suddenly shouted, her response getting lost in the thickness of her friend's sweater, the weight of her stomach. She sat up. 'I don't need this,' she shouted again. A horrible sobbing began to shake Pat's body and, unable to resist, she lay on her back with her arms and legs quivering. 'I don't need this now,' she cried.

'Sshh. Be calm. Take deep breaths.' Judith ran a grubby tissue across her friend's brow.

'I am calm,' shouted Pat, pulling at the tissue, ripping it in half.

'From the diaphragm now,' Judith insisted, recalling one of her tutor's workshops. 'Feel your rib cage move. Breathe in the light. Exhale your negativity.'

Pat wonders, could she live here, on this darker, harsher coast, sleep and eat and survive? She imagines how difficult it would be, sees herself struggling, scrabbling to catch little fish, grey shrimps, or those tiny impoverished brown-shelled crabs which have no more flesh on them than a knuckle. How long would she last? Days, months, years? Would she slowly lose her grip on the world beyond the rocks and their awful challenge? Would she keep battling on, crazily imagining there to be nothing else, no alternative? Would she ignore the ocean, turn her back on its possibilities, on taking a chance, diving in, swimming out to somewhere new?

*

'If you want to be by the sea,' Melissa said, 'why don't you rent a house in Adenport?'

She was tired. She'd been up all night with her boyfriend, trying to get him to say he loved her, wanted the baby, would stay with her. She'd showed him her shiny puffed belly, her breasts swollen and threaded with veins. She'd shown him her fears, and he'd sat with his hands tucked between his thighs, too pissed and indifferent to commit.

Pat didn't want to see the bags beneath Melissa's eyes, the washed-out paleness of her skin. She didn't want her daughter to need her. 'I have to be with the elements,' she stuttered. 'I don't want to rent a house next to other houses and hotels and bed-and-breakfast bungalows and shops which sell ice cream and sticks of rock and beach hats. I want seclusion, wildness. I have to get away.'

'Please stop this, Mum,' Melissa begged.

Pat stumbles over the rocks. It is difficult, more than difficult. The heavy grey sky is darkening, moving from dusk to night. Pat climbs and treads the unaccommodating terrain, feeling her way with her feet, one hand, whilst in the other she holds a torch. She stops briefly, leans against a boulder, shines the torch's pale yellow beam at the sea.

The tide is coming in. The long, low waves push up the shore. They are coloured petrol blue and move rhythmically, persistent. A gull floats on the water, its orange-circled eye winking.

When Pat reaches the sea, she steps into it, feels it pool around her feet, tenderly lick the chunky soles of her boots. She breathes in the air. Its smell is non-committal. There could be a storm later on, or it could improve. Pat is unable to tell.

Judith accompanied Melissa to most of her antenatals, to those intrusive, personal sessions where she was weighed, examined and tested. Melissa would have preferred her mother's support, but Pat couldn't give it – she was too busy preparing for the island and was still too sick. She tried to make the first, she sat with Melissa on the bus, but couldn't budge once the hospital came into view. Melissa alighted, pleading with Pat to join her. The bus sped off with Pat still on it, watching her daughter as she trod a circle on the pavement. Pat recognized Melissa's confusion, the horrid mess of feelings which prompted her to walk round and round and round. But there was nothing she could do.

When Pat got home she phoned Judith to tell her what had happened. She cried. She didn't mean to. And all Judith could offer was some talk about dreams. 'You may find the solution there,' she murmured. 'They are the route to your subconscious. Write them down. Think about them.' Her voice sounded hesitant, unsure, but Pat did as she suggested. She wrote about the dream she'd had the previous night.

Pat and Melissa were doing the washing up. Melissa was five. She stood on a chair with a tea towel in her hands, drying the plates as Pat passed them to her. She was asking questions, why questions. 'Why have I only one grandma and one grandpa?' she asked.

Pat stopped washing, stood with her arms in the suds. 'Just because . . . ' she replied.

'Just because what?' Melissa persisted.

Pat fished for the dishcloth and said eventually, 'I have no parents.' She wrapped the cloth around the taps. 'If I had parents then you'd have another grandpa and grandma.'

'Oh,' said Melissa. 'That's sad.'

'I know,' said Pat. 'It is sad.'

'But you have me,' offered Melissa. She looked up at her mother, puckering her sensitive lips, wanting to give her a kiss.

Pat pulled the dishcloth tight. The water flowed from it into the sink. 'That's you finished,' she said.

Pat switches off her torch, listens to the movement of the waves. Her head is thick with thoughts, the usual thoughts, the indistinct, indecipherable thoughts which fill her with panic, which bind and trap her. She feels very alone. She feels muddled and alone. She drops her torch at her feet, stretches out her arms. She moves her fingers, and senses nothing but absence, the theft of something, her loss.

A wave knocks the torch against Pat's ankles, pulls the sand from beneath her boots. And somewhere far away Pat's granddaughter wakes and Pat fails to hear the infant's sharp and startled cries. They do not blow in across the ocean. And neither does the vision of her best friend, well-meaning Judith, who cradles the baby whilst whispering to Melissa, soothing the girl with promises, condolences.

The entrance to Pat's cave is enormous. It is black and wide and gapes. Hungrily, it sucks in bird feathers, sand, ropes of seaweed, the wind. Squalls whip around the mouth like mini tornadoes. They howl. They squeal. They usher in chill and ice, a sharp uncaring frostiness which settles on Pat's belongings, her plastic dustbin and her rusted Primus, which taps on the warped and unlocked door of her wooden shelter.

Envy at the Cheese Handout

A queue forms outside the community centre. A queue of mothers and babies, old men and women, people in wheel-chairs or hobbling on sticks. It is cold, the end of November. The queue shivers, and blows a cloud of icy breath.

It's not much warmer inside. I've had to kill the heat to pre-vent the cheese and butter from spoiling. I replace the board over the centre's broken window, and turn to see the volun-teers huddled together. They've kept on their coats and mittens, headscarves and hats, but still they tremble.

My assistant is with them. She's nodding her head, listen-ing to their gripes. She's good at this. She's young. She's generous. 'I'm sorry,' she says. 'I'll put on a tape. That'll warm things up. You can stamp your feet to Van the Man.'

'Van Morrison!' snorts one of the volunteers. He wears a leather beanie and yellow trousers. He's physically unsettling.

'It's either him or Cliff Richard.' I smile and lay a hand on my assistant's shoulder. She has a slim frame, but a powerful back. I cup the solid muscle, press it gently.

My digital beeps. It is twelve o'clock. 'It's time, you bas-tards,' urges a man from outside. I think it's Mr Claythorpe. His voice distinctive, a breathy asthmatic's. His weak fists knock on the locked door and the sound prompts the volun-teers. They take out their pens and spiral bound notepads. They edge towards the trestle tables.

'Well,' I say to Fyona. 'Here we go.'

I'm a graduate. I went to college to escape from home. I packed my bags and travelled two hundred miles north and my parents waved me off willingly, happily, because they thought I would succeed. Instead I drank cheap wine, had sex with lazy art students and filed bad memories.

I scraped an ordinary degree and walked from one institution into another. The Department of Health and Social Security. 1980. I wanted it that way. I had no ambitions, no plans. I thought life on the dole would be like college but better.

It was fine during the summer, I went for walks. But winter was different. The snow and gales kept me indoors. I crouched by the Calor gas heater, lying on my side to warm my back, on all fours to warm my face, my feet. The heater stank and ate my money. I looked for work. But nothing doing. Too inexperienced. Too few jobs. Wrong kind of face. Too fresh and green.

I was on the dole for three years. I kept my dole money in a jam jar, so I could see what little I had. Every second Tuesday was the worst. The day before I received my giro. The day when I'd scrat along the skirting, under the sofa, behind the cooker. Looking for a lost coin.

They were grey years with no landmarks or high spots except for the food handouts. The free EEC cheese and butter. I can still feel its weight, two pounds of butter, two large lumps of cheese, heavy in my carrier bag. The butter was too yellow, the cheese too orange, but that didn't matter. They were wrapped in thick clean greaseproof like classy packages from a delicatessen. I placed their precious bodies in the fridge and the creamy fridge light embraced them.

I unbolt the community centre door. It's not much of a door. It's made of plywood and has been axed by the neighbourhood villains. Three times they've chopped through to thieve petty cash and toilet rolls. The council won't give me a metal one which can be secured by padlocks and pins. The council only does what it wants to do, choosing to protect the green belt and banning dogs from the crematorium, granting permission for food handouts when refusing wouldn't be politic.

The door swings back and I fix it with a stop. 'Good morning, Mr Claythorpe,' I say to the old man as he edges past. His

33

walking stick gets caught in the tatty lino and he coughs an obscenity.

He is followed by a trail of people, mostly slumped, carrying empty carrier bags and dole cards. 'Good morning. Good morning,' I smile, cheery because it's my job. I'm supposed to bring people together, to give this horrible area a focal point, a meeting place, somewhere to feel less lonely. I'm not that successful. People are wary of me.

Even Mrs Robertson, who I see on my way to work, who I spoke to this morning as she swept her street. Even she circumvents me. She's doing it now. Keeping a yard between us as she heads for the surplus. Because I'm an outsider. I don't come from the estate.

The Butler Estate which gets into the Sunday supplements, because it looks like a holiday camp. A pink and blue prefab land which houses the unemployed, the single parents, the sick and elderly. 'Hell In Heaven,' say the supplements. 'Hi-De-Hi to the Low-De-Lows.'

When I was small I thought the world a magical place. My bedroom was peach and pink. My toys were soft and cuddly. I believed in Santa. I believed in fairies and elves, pixies, angels, God.

Primary school opened my eyes. The teachers with their hang-ups: Mrs Smartly with her big round bottom moving between the tables, smacking her hand across Tony Jones' back, his face, his thin legs. Something was wrong with Tony Jones, but Mrs Smartly didn't want to know. She bullied him till he flipped. I huddled in the school playground with the rest of my form listening to Tony Jones wrecking the classroom. Weedy Tony Jones overturning the sand pit, the Wendy house, the desks, the book corner, crapping in Mrs Smartly's handbag.

The first time I met Brian I told him about Tony. We were queuing for our free EEC cheese and butter and we got talking. We talked sincerely, naïvely, and agreed the world needed changing. We persuaded each other to try for community work. I will if you will. I will right some wrongs if you will.

I had stopped believing in fairies, but I still believed bad could be turned to good. When I look at Fyona I see myself as I was back then.

Fyona steers a volunteer towards me. Her arm is raised and she directs energetically. She's always projecting. She never spends quiet moments thinking about herself. She whizzes around like a character in a cartoon. Her legs in a spin, her face smiley smiley.

'Excuse me, Cathy,' says Fyona. 'Simon's here to help with the queue.'

'Right,' I reply.

Fyona says goodbye to Simon and then hurries off. I watch her as she takes a carton from one of the older volunteers. 'Hup,' she says, lifting the box of food on to his trestle table. She runs a hand across her brow, pretending to mop sweat. The volunteer laughs and pats her back.

I address Simon. 'Just keep them from wandering. A nice orderly line against the wall.'

Simon nods his bobble-hatted head. A neat head with huge brown eyes. A handsome head. I've seen him before. In the summer he saunters round town wearing a skinny rib T-shirt and skimpy shorts. You can see what he's about. He's scouting. And he's doing it here. A selfish volunteer, like most volunteers, in it for the return.

He gently ushers the queue, his eyes assessing every woman. He seems to prefer the rare alternative types. Women who eat nothing but vegetables and ride bikes. Women with taut bodies and short stubbly hair. He cheeks one. He lays his head on his shoulder, grins his tiny-mouthed grin.

We had the Healthy Heart Roadshow at the centre last week. Two district nurses with enormous breasts and sturdy legs, dressed in white overalls, set up a clinic. Anybody could attend. It was to create awareness. Too many people are dying from heart disease on the Butler Estate, and it's costing the health service.

They mounted display boards covered with gory pictures. Pictures of our most precious organ bloated and twisted, shrivelled and clogged. Pictures of young men and women lying comatose on hospital beds with tubes up their noses.

'See what can happen,' said the district nurses. 'If you don't eat right, drink sensibly, walk every day.' They took blood samples, handed out diet sheets, sat Mr Claythorpe on an exercise bicycle and made him pedal till his face turned blue.

I asked them about the food handout. 'It seems a little cruel,' I said. 'You show fat can kill, and then the government doles out lumps of butter and processed cheese, no charge. What do people do?' The district nurses shrugged their shoulders: conundrums weren't their bag.

The queue feeds past the trestle tables. The first table is for registration, the second for collecting the cheese, the third for collecting the butter. Sometimes there is a fourth table on which are stacked tins of minced beef. But not today. Because Marjorie is in charge today and she refuses to deal with the beef. She's no vegetarian. She feels uncertain about handing out meat which is scarlet and smells of creosote.

Marjorie is the area co-ordinator for EEC handouts. She organizes the venues, the publicity, the shifting and stocking of food. She selects and trains the volunteers. She is efficient and professional.

I quite like her, though she's the opposite of Fyona. She hasn't much compassion. She told me once that she can't afford to feel sorry for people, because people take advantage. Especially poor people, people who are on the edge. 'Give them an inch,' she said.

Marjorie is on the registration desk. She checks the claimants' dole cards. She's looking for fraudsters, those who are taking a mile. 'Sorry,' she says to a young woman. She holds the tatty UB40 between a finger and thumb, and flaps it disdainfully. 'But you've already collected. Last month. Your card has been stamped. I'm afraid you're not entitled.'

'But . . .' says the woman. She jiggles a baby on her hip. The baby is nine or ten months old. It has rosy cheeks, rosy from teething or rosy from the cold. 'But I've been queuing for the past hour. My arms are breaking. I wouldn't be doing this if I wasn't desperate.'

'Sorry,' says Marjorie. 'But rules are rules. I sympathize with your situation, but I cannot give you more than your fair share. Lots of people are desperate. You are not alone.'

'Well I feel fucking alone,' says the young woman, jiggling her baby furiously. The baby begins to cry. 'Well I feel fucking alone.'

Fyona watches children's television. She says it's got balance. It shows the world is a sad place, but a happy place too. It helps you to smile and thank your lucky stars. She especially likes *Newsround*, where even pictures of starving babes are made upbeat. 'They run this horrible film,' she says, 'but then they give you details of how you can help by knitting some squares or saving tinfoil. Nothing is hopeless. There's always a solution.'

Newsround told her about the food schemes which they run in America. Where food which has passed its sell-by date or food wrapped in damaged packaging is given to the poor. Chicago. The home of gangsters and the home of good will. Fyona applauded the fat charity worker as he delivered boxes of groceries to black family after black family.

Sometimes I blank when Fyona enthuses, or sometimes I challenge her. She doesn't like being challenged. It makes her tense. It makes her eyes water. I don't know why I do it, because it's not great seeing someone lose their breeze. I asked her if *Newsround* mentioned how dangerous it was to eat old and damaged food. 'What about botulism?' I asked.

The queue is thinning. I remove the stop from the door and push it to.

'Good idea,' says a woman huddled inside an old army coat, the heavy shapeless sort with brass buttons and wide lapels. She has a knitted hat pulled over her ears and looks like an extra in a war movie or dramatized documentary about down and outs.

I smile at the woman and edge past her. A small child clings to the hem of her coat. The child has a red nose and smells of vapour rub.

Children make me awkward. Brian has three. Lucy, Edward and Vanessa. Their round faces and strange noises start me humming. Desperate tunes. 'Please Release Me'. 'Heaven Knows I'm Miserable Now'. 'San Quentin'.

Children split us up. Brian wanted them. I didn't. He said he needed to be a proper daddy. He said he couldn't parent the lost and the lonely, the despairing of Butler Estate. Not any more. He jacked in community work and crept from our bed.

Night after night I phoned him. I begged him to return, to regrow his ponytail, to dig out his jacket with the CND symbol chalked on the back. Night after night I pleaded for the old days. But he told me to grow up, and I cried.

We are friendly now. Courteous. Civil. I help pack his groceries in the back of his Volvo when we bump into each other at the supermarket and I try to smile at his children sitting strapped in their car seats. I haven't met his wife. Fyona has. She says she's nice-looking, with soft grey eyes and a soft soft voice. 'Not like me, then?' I asked.

Fyona invited a fortune teller to come to the centre. Tina Tinsella. She arrived with her tarot cards and her bag of runes and a small collapsible table. She set up in the main hall, and one by one the teenage mums from the Unsupported Mothers'

Group and the men and women from the Drugs Initiative queued for a forecast.

'You are at a crossroads,' Tinsella told me. 'In your past life you lived in Ireland, had two children and you wrote stories. You died when you were thirty-four. How old are you now?'

'Thirty-four,' I said.

'That is why you're at a crossroads,' she replied.

Tina Tinsella charged £50.00 for the day, and I deducted it from Fyona's wages. She didn't mind. She knows I have to keep the books straight and our budget doesn't stretch to fancies like Tinsella. And money means nothing to Fyona as long as she can give her mum some board and pay her annual sub to Rouge.

Who was the EEC bigwig with the golden heart, the one who persuaded the other bigwigs that handing out the surplus would be better, more expedient, more humane than letting it rot, than letting the butter turn rancid, the cheese moulder?

How much of the surplus is given away?

How much remains piled mountain high in giant EEC coolers, sheds and warehouses?

Why butter and cheese and sometimes minced beef? Why not pasta and lamb and mayonnaise?

Why not charge a nominal sum, say one pence for each item, and give the money to Children In Need?

Why give free food away to Europeans when there are millions starving in Africa?

Fyona has produced a fact sheet which answers all these questions and more. She's put a stack on the registration table and people are shoving them in their carrier bags.

They'll not be appreciated. They'll be scanned for a money off coupon or a free prize draw and they'll be discarded. When I first started work here I wrote a sheet about the centre's limited facilities. I called it WHAT WE CAN OFFER YOU. The whole pile disappeared within the week and I felt encouraged. Then I found a wad on top of the condom machine. About thirty sheets, each one defaced with marker pen. 'Ping-pong isn't sex,' said the graffiti, 'Single parents want money not advice' and 'Job Clubs delude'.

It is nearly five o'clock. Boxes litter the centre floor. Blocks of butter and cheese tumble from cartons, off trestle tables. A hillock of lost items builds by the exit – benefit cards, glasses, scarves, a pair of false teeth, a Swiss army knife.

'Phone,' shouts Fyona, signalling to me from our small office. The office has a doorway but no door. Fyona stands in the opening, framed like a still from an arty movie.

I squeeze past her, my body brushing her knobbly hips, her flat stomach. Her jeans are too big and she's pulled them in with a large brown belt. She looks agricultural. 'Who is it?' I ask.

'Pensioners Action Group,' she replies.

She smiles, then leaves the office to help Marjorie flush out the remaining claimants. I pick up the phone and say 'Yes.'

'PAG here,' says Mr Claythorpe. His asthmatic breath whistling down the line.

Brian and I studied at college for our CW badges. Our favourite lecturer was Tom. A kindly ageing man who told Good Samaritan stories. 'Heard the one about the disabled sailor and the tramp?' he would say.

'No,' we'd lie.

I used to talk to Tom a lot. And when he died I continued to talk to him. I visited the bowling green where his ashes were scattered, knelt close to the glossy turf which his body fed, and confided my thoughts, my hopes, my dreams.

But not any more. The affinity's gone.

Some days I walk past the club, hear the soft whooshing of the untroubled bowls, and I want to cry. Some days I catch the sheltered sound of mower and edge clippers and want to shout.

Do you realize there are people who believe that charity

40

demotivates, that giving a helping hand breeds complacency? These people complain about the EEC handouts. They write letters to the local newspaper and phone the centre. 'I pay my taxes,' they begin. 'I've had to struggle to get where I am today. No European Economic Community gave me free food.'

Then there are people who believe they have more right than others; more right to benefits, to free food, to emergency payments, to good housing. There are people who consider their suffering to be more deserving, more painful, always top of the agony charts, never mid-league.

These people are in the majority. I battle with them every day.

The Saracen is a pub a few roads away from the centre. It is a squat building with no windows. The outside is covered with crimson panelling and stucco. The inside is tiled black. A large circular bar sits in the middle of the pub's main room. The bar is flush with wrought iron and Formica. The barman has LOVE and ANGER tattooed across his knuckles. He plays flick with a beer mat.

A poster is pinned on the bar. The poster is discoloured by cigarette smoke and drink stains. It advertises the free EEC surplus. 'You better take that down,' I say to the barman. 'The handout is finished.'

I cup my pint of thick dark Guinness. I don't like the Saracen. The lack of natural light oppresses me. I usually sit by the bar facing the open door, staring out at the evening sky. Its navy blue is preferable to the flickering hue of fluorescence. And I can smell the air, the wideness of the streets before they narrow to meet the community centre and the Butler Estate.

'You're in early tonight,' says the barman.

I nod, dip my finger in the pint's head. 'My assistant's locking up,' I explain.

'She'll be after your job. You watch it,' warns the barman.

'Mmm,' I say. 'Mmm.'

*

I gave Fyona the keys, told her I wouldn't be in tomorrow to face representatives from PAG to explain why single parents were given an extra block of cheese and not the elderly, told her I was leaving. For ever. 'It's all yours,' I said. 'I'm too old. I can't soothe the green eye, fight the good fight. I can't be bothered any more.'

'Oh,' she replied, slipping the keys in her trouser pocket. Her surprised face so clean, so open. I was close enough to see the baby fine hair which decorates her jaw and I touched it. 'Oh Cathy,' she said, as I held my hand to her. 'Oh dear.'

This morning I'd walked to work through the Butler Estate. The pink and blue prefab land. The flat-roofed, flimsy homes with their small back yards and badly fitted windows. Some of the windows were dressed with ruched curtains – red nylon extravaganzas. Some of them were double glazed with polythene. A woman moved slowly along one row of prefabs. She was crouched and held a bin bag. She wore thick mittens and patted the road with them. Mrs Robertson picking up litter. Plain Mrs Robertson with her shrunken needlecord jacket, patched jeans and dirty trainers. Circumventing Mrs Robertson.

'Hello Mrs Robertson,' I greeted. 'You're doing a good job.'
'Maybe,' she said reluctantly.

She straightened her back, watched the wind blow a bunch of chocolate wrappers past my legs. They wove through a fence towards someone's battered front porch. A jumble of cans sat on the porch and a carrier crammed with tinfoil trays and a grey chicken carcass.

'Maybe,' she said. 'Or . . . ' She waved her gloves at the unhappy scene. 'Or maybe I'm wasting my time.'

Johnny Came Courting

Gertrude Smith's husband was an opinionated man, abrasive. He worked for the civil service and went on lengthy hush hush trips to Northern Ireland. He was into hanging, firearms and rugby. He could only bring himself to kiss Gertrude in bed, in the dark, under the covers.

He died five years ago. A simple death. Gertrude woke to find him cold with his mouth slightly ajar. She studied him closely, amazed to see his cheeks were pockmarked, his nose pink-tinged and flabby like a drinker's. She realized she had never really known him, that she had been married to a stranger. Bitterly she felt for his testicles and squashed them beneath her hands. But she cried at the funeral, and for months after felt sad and strangely hollow.

She surfaced from her grief quite suddenly, like a whale breaking the ocean's skin. One minute in the depths, the next feeling the sun and the air. She stretched out her arms and determined she would enjoy herself. She took up bowls. She joined the WI and the Greenfingers Club, played bingo at the Stargazers Hall, and unknowingly she collected admirers.

Like Jim Arnold and Harry Fisher who mowed the local bowling green. Like Mrs Bartholomew, the undisputed queen of bingo. Like Mr Cox the grocer, her most ardent admirer, who throbbed with a deep yearning and believed Gertrude Smith to be his answer to everything.

He tried to make his passion known, spending entire evenings cutting the alphabet from magazines to spell words like LOVE, ADMIRE, WANT, DESIRE. He stuck these words on pink sugar paper, encircled them with shakily drawn hearts. And he sent

43

the Valentines to Gertrude Smith, who considered them a schoolgirl prank.

She threw them in her waste bin and sighed. She would like a little love, a little affection, but could not imagine anyone wanting her. At her wedding reception, the best man had described her as lovely-looking, like an angel atop a Christmas tree. He would laugh to see her now. With pigmented skin and false teeth. A size twenty, reduced to buying shapeless dresses from a street-market trader named Desmond.

Mrs Bartholomew, Jim Arnold and Harry Fisher sensed Gertrude's insecurity. They realized wooing her would require persuasion, cajoling, too much effort. So they preferred to keep their distance, to dream. Mr Cox was different.

Mr Cox had spent a lifetime with his head stuck in crates of fruit. He had poured rice, flour and oats into brown paper bags, set them in neat lines on the shelves behind his shop counter. He had ordered stock cubes, tins of peas, jars of jam. He had stuck special offer labels on roasting bags. He had never felt a burning passion. He had never kissed.

It might have been the hot weather, the humid breeze blowing around his shop. It might have been the phone call from his brother telling him he was emigrating. It might have been the newspaper articles about the failed Rio Earth Summit. It might have been his birth certificate found beneath a stack of old till rolls. Whatever, it suddenly hit him that he had never really experienced anything. And when Gertrude Smith came into his shop, barely out of her widow's black, smiling a warm and overwhelming smile, he saw opportunity, a chance to live.

But Mr Cox was shy. Each time he served Gertrude he opened his mouth to ask her to accompany him to the pictures and only managed to say, 'That'll be ten pounds seventy please.' He became quite aggravated. To be incapacitated when all he ever wanted was before him. Miserably, he glued his anonymous Valentines. Hoping Gertrude Smith would guess the sender. Hoping she would enter his shop one day and register the wanting that lay behind his shopkeeper smile.

Gertrude Smith had been a customer of Mr Cox's for years. The shop reassured her. She could look along Mr Cox's shelves and know she would find tinned pineapple nuzzling tinned raspberries, dishcloths next to detergent. And she liked the personal service, Mr Cox's deference. 'Mr Courtesy Cox,' her husband used to call him. 'Mr Courtesy Cox, our friendly neighbourhood ingratiate.'

Mrs Gertrude Smith could not say when she began to feel uneasy about Mr Cox, uneasy about entering his shop. The feeling built gradually. It was like watching a good thriller on TV. Everything seemed so very normal, except it wasn't. There was an undercurrent: a tension in Mr Cox's smile, a quivering when he placed her groceries in their brown paper bags. 'Are you all right?' she asked him when he dropped one of her peaches on the floor. A peach she had personally selected and had studied for blemishes. A peach she had stroked, because peach skin reminded her of babies. The babies she'd wanted but had never been given.

Mr Cox cherished the words 'Are you all right?' He took them upstairs to his flat, whispered them aloud, mouthed them to his reflection in his shaving mirror. He was disappointed that he didn't sound like Gertrude. He was unable to change the gruffness of his voice. He couldn't get the upward lilt of her Rs. He had read in one of his courting manuals about flattery. Flattery was the key to winning a woman's heart. Imitation being the sincerest form.

Mr Cox had thought about imitating Gertrude Smith. He had thought about buying one of her flowery dresses from Desmond. But when he couldn't match the lilt of her voice he gave up. He sat at his kitchen table cutting words of passion from the local freesheet, wondering how to break through his shyness and court Gertrude proper.

*

The first week in October was sultry. The sky shone a bright unnatural blue and Gertrude Smith felt sweaty as she trudged up the cemetery path. She carried a small plastic watering can, a trowel and a bag of bulbs. She was visiting her husband's grave, on the anniversary of his death.

As she bent to dig in the bulbs, the sun pasted Gertrude's polyester dress to her back. Mr Cox watched her from behind an ostentatious headstone. It was a well-known headstone, a representation of a love knot, over six feet high and carved in pearly granite. It marked the grave of a spinster poet and her faithful housekeeper.

Mr Cox stroked the love knot, unaware that it was a love knot, absorbed in Gertrude Smith. He watched her body heavily swaying, her large arched back, her comfortable backside blocking the view to her husband's stone. Mr Cox felt faint with wanting. His penis, which had lain curled and tired for years, now began to stir, began to inspire.

It was a drastic idea, and yet it wasn't. It wasn't as drastic as opening his mouth and asking for some time, attention and warmth. He thought the message oblique enough to save him from the embarrassment of a face-to-face rejection, to save him from dreadful hurt. He thought he could turn it into a joke if it seemed it was failing. Drastic but cleverly obscure. A half way step.

Gertrude had had a bad morning. The menopause was not being kind to her. A rush of blood had stained her sheets, reminding her of younger times, making her feel cheated. She walked to Mr Cox the grocer's with a head full of longing. She almost stopped at the newsagent's to buy a paperback romance. She almost stopped at the florist's to buy herself a bunch of flowers, so she could place them on her sideboard and pretend they were a gift from a *beau*.

At first she didn't notice the small multicoloured box placed next to Mr Cox's till. She didn't even notice Mr Cox's agitation which was extreme. He shifted behind the counter like a man with shingles. Frantically he ran his hands through his thinning hair. 'Yes?' he bleated when Gertrude came close, pushing the multicoloured box within her sight.

Gertrude Smith checked her shopping list. She was beginning to feel her usual uneasiness. She really couldn't be doing with it. Everything was out of kilter. Her womb ached and her favourite shop no longer soothed her. She considered changing her life. An own-brand supermarket had opened close by. It was bright, shiny and sterile, and the shop assistants functioned like automatons.

'Yes? Yes?' squeaked Mr Cox, unable to contain his excitement. He had dreamt about this moment since the graveyard. He had convinced himself he'd found the answer. A little something to surprise Gertrude Smith, to make her view him differently, to make her see him as a man. Mr Cox removed one of the condoms from the multicoloured box and flapped it in the air.

Gertrude Smith looked up from her shopping list. In the gloom of the shop she couldn't quite see what Mr Cox was doing. She thought perhaps he'd won a lottery or a raffle. He was jigging like a maniac as he waved a scrap of silver from left to right, left to right. 'What is it, Mr Cox?' she asked. 'Have you got the jackpot?'

Mr Cox couldn't speak. He suddenly wondered if Gertrude was simple. Her husband had said so often enough. He ripped the foil packet and popped the condom on the end of his pinkie. He waggled it like a finger puppet. 'Here. Here,' he almost shouted, but didn't.

Because he realized he'd gone too far. He'd lost his decorum and had wounded Gertrude. He wasn't insensitive. He could tell from the way her hefty shoulders slumped, the shaking of her proud and homely head.

Desmond moved into Mr Cox's. He stripped the shop of its wooden interior, replaced the oak with plastic shelving. He

47

sanded down the counter and painted it a vivid green. He gutted upstairs. He piled Mr Cox's books on how to charm, his scissored magazines, in a skip. He pulled up the orange-swirled carpet, ripped out his bath, unscrewed his shaving mirror. Downstairs became a video store and the little bed-sitter a poster emporium. A life-sized picture of Madonna hung in the corner where Mr Cox's trouser press used to be.

Gertrude Smith never returned to the grocer's and only learnt about its transformation at the Greenfingers Club. She shivered when Mr Cox was mentioned, but agreed wholeheartedly that his day was done, that the own-brand supermarket was more convenient and cheaper and its range of TV dinners for one inspired. She couldn't admit the wide spacious aisles disorientated her and the muzak made her sad.

Helping Fiona

It is 8.00 a.m. Sylvester packs his black bag, brushes his hair, buttons his fly. He opens his living-room curtains, looks out of his window across the road.

He stares at the disused and derelict docks, the dry wrecked basins, the huge discoloured troughs which gape beneath the city sky. Nothing stirs.

The stillness is frightening, though it is the same every morning. The barren hush which hangs in the air, which seems to fix the docks, to confirm the land as wasted and lost. Sylvester can feel its icy cold. He can smell it.

A bus passes and obscures his view. The vehicle's jaunty yellow reminds him: it is summer. Briefly Sylvester thinks of the seaside, of sand and buckets and spades and plastic windmills, then he registers the broken glass, the litter from last night's fight lying close to the dockyard wall.

Sylvester was in bed when he heard the men. Grunting and groaning they crawled under the broken security fence to stagger round the flat lip of the nearest basin. The docks are regularly used as a place to settle scores, to work off drink, drugs and blinding curries. Sylvester waited for the usual sounds of fists hitting flesh, of heads meeting heads.

'Ugh,' cried the men, as they laid into each other.

'Aaargh,' screamed a youngster as he was flung against the wall.

The wall divides one side of the docks from a clutch of smaller businesses, businesses which are still alive, which are struggling on though the premises are wrecked, the customers few. It's an enormous wall, wide and threaded with alcoves.

The thick smack alarmed Sylvester. He sat up and his pulse began to speed. The gang was moving towards the wall. He

49

sensed the men hunching forward, edging towards the youngster, edging towards Fiona.

He daren't look to see if Fiona was there, if the men had
discovered her curled in her hole. And he put his fingers in his
ears when the laughter began, a raucous laughter which inter-
mingled with the horrible sound of female bleating, the sad
soft pule of the fairer sex.

Sylvester spies Fiona's feet. They stick out from her pitch in
the wall, and appear as fixed as the docks, but also vulnerable.
Small teenage feet, dressed in black pumps, pointing upwards.
Sylvester hopes she is all right.

It is cutting him up, this caring for Fiona. And he has no one
to share it with. His pain and confusion swirl inside him,
making him fearful, making him wretched.

Fiona's body is a strong body. It swallows blows like a double-
stitched cushion. It has been stabbed, slashed, strangled,
fucked. It received the men last night without any trouble.
Fiona should be grateful for her body, but she isn't.

When all the hassle started she wished for a weak frame,
internal organs which would burst, skin which would blister
and flake, limbs which would drop off or get gangrene, or just
shrivel, a body which would die. But luck has never been with
Fiona. Luck gave her a sturdy body and an unsturdy mind.

Her mind was fine at first. It let her enjoy life, laugh at jokes,
make friends, pass exams. But then it started to tell her things,
things she didn't want to hear. It started badgering her. It
made her doubtful. It made her question, requestion, question
again. Did I really do that? Did that really happen? Did I really
do that? Did I?

Nighttime was the worst. Her dreams made her scream.
She would wake screaming and sweating and shaking. She
couldn't tell you what her dreams were about. They usually
involved somewhere dark. A shed. Perhaps a chicken shed or
a doocot. There was a terrible scratching and shuffling and
ruffling of birds, and the sound of someone human beside

herself, someone standing close to her with acid-smelling breath. Light breaths. In. Out. In. Out.

Fiona hasn't had these dreams in a long time. Not since she started drinking, not since she started obliterating. Her sleep is a thick black fugue, and she is grateful for it.

Though it always hurts when she wakes. Because mornings bring clarity. She can taste, smell, see, feel in the mornings. She is open and vulnerable in the mornings, and increasingly the mornings have brought bad news.

Fiona shifts in her hole. She can hear Sylvester. His voice floats over the docks, carries like gentle bird call.

'Here I am. Syl . . . ves . . . ter!' sings his voice. 'Syl . . . ves . . . ter. Your min . . . der!'

Fiona rolls on her side, waking from safe oblivion to the sudden smell of air – not so fresh – of water – not so clean – of earth – concreted and covered in piss. She peeps through one bruised eye, sees a blurry crisp packet, a valiant tuft of grass.

She grunts, turning on to her back, closing her eye tight to the grey never-ending sky, padding her hand on the ground beside her, searching for her bottle.

Sylvester started visiting Fiona last December. When he first appeared, pretending to knock on her alcove like a gentleman chapping a lady's front door, she thought he was a bad one. Too many men have visited as she's been lying out of it, ill and wrecked. Too many men have entered her hole without invitation, have barged their way in and barged their way out again. She shivered when she saw Sylvester, his large body bending down to look at her. She tried to make herself vomit because sick puts most men off. She hunched her shoulders, rammed her fingers down her throat and retched.

'That's a bit silly now,' said Sylvester. 'You've dirtied your home.'

When he asked to be her minder, she nodded. She nodded because she couldn't say no. She nodded and waited for him to deliver the crunch. But he's not stuck his hand out for money. He's not pestered for sex. He's not pulled down her pants to take photos of her crack.

And over the weeks, over the months, he's just cared for her. Like a little mother.

Fiona lifts her head to greet Sylvester. He stands close to her and she could kiss his feet if she wanted. The scuffed toes of his trainers tap beside her mouth.

'Oh Fiona,' says Sylvester from above. His reedy voice works through her bunged and bruised ears. 'What a mess,' he says.

Sylvester puts his oblong hands beneath Fiona's arms, pulls her from her tunnel. 'There you go,' he murmurs, moving his head away from her gasp, the salty sweet breath which flicks under his nose.

'Huh,' Fiona slumps against his leg. She's a strange-looking girl. Worn out but still fresh. With soft skin and a young shape.

Sylvester opens his black bag to remove a toothbrush and toothpaste, a damp flannel and a brown and orange striped towel. He begins to clean Fiona, as he does most mornings.

He wipes the flannel over Fiona's face, but doesn't ask her about the marks, about the blue and black bumps beneath her eyes, the cut on her lip, the finger-shaped depressions around her throat. Too much concern would panic her.

He lets his hand rest a while, feeling her nose through the cloth. She has a pert nose, a cheeky nose. Sylvester feels the nose, tries not to imagine the scene last night, then gently twists the flannel to blow and catch the thick mucus which gathers in her nostrils.

'Bit clogged today,' Sylvester comments.

'Mmm,' says Fiona.

Sylvester folds the flannel and returns it to his bag. He hands Fiona the towel, and she clumsily pats herself dry while Sylvester squirts a streak of toothpaste on a slim yellow brush.

Fiona opens her mouth. Sylvester takes her puffy chin in

one hand. He uses the other to run the toothbrush across her wide even teeth. He is very thorough with her teeth. He brushes and brushes and brushes, and occasionally he catches her gums, making them bleed.

Fiona's parents are hairdressers. They run a salon from the front room of their detached house. They are a formidable team. Fiona's mother specializes in perms and sets: she bonds with the pensioners. Fiona's father does a nice feather cut and a short back and sides. In the good old days Fiona would help them. She'd select the rollers, sweep up the dead hair, take appointments, make coffee.

Sometimes Fiona gets a very clear picture of her mother. She is standing at the salon window, her high-rise hairdo pushing aside the curtain. She is very still, watching the yellow double-deckers travel along the road. A scrawny woman with a large backside, the top button of her skirt usually undone, showing a bit of her nylon slip, usually pink.

The image sometimes comes to Fiona first thing. It's a picture postcard image. A photo from long ago. When the image appears Fiona shakes her head, sending it back to her archive of memories: the archive which holds images worse than this one, images which aren't as easy to dispose of, images which have started to flash.

Quick and painful. Intruding into her mornings, and sometimes her afternoons.

Images which she sees the bottom of or the top of or a corner of, but never the whole. Never the whole.

A fat man. She can tell. His fat feet splayed. His ankles puffed and swollen.

Sylvester's heart flips. Fiona whimpers and he thinks he has hurt her. 'Sorry,' he says. 'Sorry. Sorry.'

Tenderly, he straightens Fiona, props her against the lip of her hole. As he does so, he spies a brown stain drawing a curve across Fiona's backside. The smell is cat-strong, pungent, whistling sharp up Sylvester's nostrils.

Fiona is one of the cleaner drunks. She tries hard not to piss or shit herself, and when she was still having her periods she would make sure she had some protection, a handkerchief, a cloth, tissues, toilet roll, or – luxury – sanitary towels lifted from Boots. Sometimes though, especially if she's had a bad session, especially if she's been bashed and kicked, her track-suit bottoms are bogging. Like today.

Sylvester returns the toiletries to his bag, then removes a small calendar. He flicks over the calendar, pretending to trace his finger along the dates. 'Time you had a bath, Fiona,' he says.

'Had one last week.'

'Not according to my calendar,' smiles Sylvester.

Fiona takes a bath a month. Sylvester believes this is necessary and Fiona seems to agree. But it is her limit. When Sylvester tried to get her to bathe more she threw a fit. She held her breath, made her face blow purple and red. Sylvester thought he was losing her, and now if Fiona needs an additional scrub he just lies. He pretends the weeks have sped by, that it is a new month – May instead of April, August instead of July. He pretends her regular bath is due. Sylvester thinks this is fair, not too dishonest of him, justifiable.

Sylvester's flat is a small tenement flat on the top floor. Sylvester swears the flat has been refurbished inside, but it looks mouldy old to Fiona. Even her blurred eyes can't soften the stains, the peeling wallpaper, the dingy drabness.

The doors are covered in the thick red and brown paint of long ago. A maroon stripe runs around the hall walls – a crusty Victorian border. The bed-recess leading off the kitchen is still a bed-recess and hasn't been transformed into a shower or a dining area and Sylvester still sleeps there, using a curtain drawn across the mouth to cut out the cooking smells. Only the bathroom looks modern. The suite is green – 'Pampas

Grass' boasts Sylvester – the taps are shiny monoblocs, and the toilet has a push-down flush.

The flat is Sylvester's. He inherited it from his mother. She bought it before he was born, when she wasn't so troubled.

Sylvester likes the flat. He likes the freedom it gives him – no landlords, no rent books. He likes knowing it is his and he will always have it. He likes the memories which linger in the decor, which flood from cupboards when he opens them, which sit in the household fluff and dust and cobwebs. He likes all this and then he doesn't. Some days he feels his mother left him a prison, a personal space which he can never escape.

It is better though when Fiona visits – her feet treading his carpets, her hands touching his walls. She changes things. She brings a future to his home, she seems to fit.

The bathroom extractor fan whirs above Fiona's head. The noise is comforting. A consistent hum which blurs the sound of her body moving in the water.

Fiona doesn't like hearing her body. She doesn't like feeling it. She doesn't like seeing it.

She bathes with her eyes shut. If she needs the soap or the flannel she squints and occasionally fumbles with her fingers, blanching if she touches her skin.

At first Sylvester used to wash her. He'd strip her and lift her into the hot bath. But even though he was discreet and gentle she could not bear him doing this, and once she vomited in the water as he moved the flannel across her stomach. Now she braves the washing on her own. Sylvester stands outside the bathroom, an ear pressed against the bobbled glass door, while Fiona pats, dabs and wipes her body in disgust.

'Are you all right in there?' asks Sylvester.

He hears the splish splash of Fiona stepping from the bath. The sound reminds him of the water he trickled on his mother's forehead. He used a sponge to do it, a bright pink sponge which he hoped his mother could see, though her senses were almost gone and she didn't seem to register light or sound or smells. She just lay there on the hospital bed exuding heat, a sticky moisture he couldn't swill away. On her last day she sucked on the pink sponge, and its vivid colour mocked her grey lips, her ashen skin. It repulsed Sylvester. It made him want to weep.

Fiona dries herself. Sylvester observes her movements, the outline of Fiona's body through the bathroom door. He'd felt uneasy when he'd had to undress and bath Fiona. It had been a relief when she'd asked him to stay outside.

'I'll go and get your drink then, if you're all right,' Sylvester says. He lays a finger on the glass. Fiona's image flutters beneath it. The door is between them; if it wasn't he'd be touching her hair. His finger would be pushing through her brutal crop. He wonders if she's shampooed it, washed away the spit and the smell of last night. Then he heads for his kitchen.

Fiona sits on Sylvester's comfy couch. She wears Sylvester's dressing gown, his slippers styled to look like frogs. She moves her feet and the frogs appear to jump on the worn patchy carpet.

'You OK?' asks Sylvester, entering the living room. He hands Fiona a large gin and she sinks it quick.

'More,' she says, staring at him. She holds out the mug, and shivers. The shiver tips the mug this way and that, fast and jerky.

She's feeling bad today. The steamy bath has sifted through her skull. She can see too much. Her mind feels too breezy, too jaunty, too cheeky. She's waiting for it to play a trick. Remember this one?

Fingers. A big man's fingers.

Fiona moans. Sylvester grabs the mug. 'Oh give it here,' he

says. He hates giving booze to Fiona. He wants to be done with it. But he knows it's too soon, that Fiona needs more time.

He shuffles into the kitchen, reluctantly reaches for the bottle sitting on top of his fridge.

Fiona clutches the dressing gown tighter. She listens for the sound of a bottle cap turning, alcohol pouring into a tea mug. She can locate the sounds even though the washing machine is in full spin and her tracksuit zip is battering the machine's glass dome door.

Sylvester shouts from the kitchen. 'Do you want to go up the town? If we get your clothes dry?'

'Mmm.' Fiona tries to stand, to walk her froggy feet from her memories. And as she stands she sees Sylvester framed in the doorway. The wakening summer sun sends a muddy glow through the kitchen window. It traces him, flickers through his wispy hair. It makes him look fragile. Like a flimsy decoration, a paper cut-out. Which can be screwed up, torn in two.

Noon, and the city centre is wild. Heat haze shimmers at either end of the main street's pedestrianized stretch. Crowds of tourists buzz in between, flowing from the busy shops, stopping to applaud the buskers, the born again Christian preaching through his loudhailer, the pavement artist chalking James Dean in the doorway of John Menzies. Tubs of exuberant flowers sit beside benches crammed with old ladies and toddlers licking ice creams. Banners advertising the Visual Arts Festival flap from lampposts and flagpoles. And a biplane trails a thin line of white smoke through the clear blue sky.

Sylvester steers Fiona off the double-decker. She stumbles as she treads the space mid bus and pavement. 'Fuck,' she says.

'Never mind,' soothes Sylvester. He links her arm through his and turns the corner into the shoppers' paradise.

Fiona is up to high doh. The gin is whizzing round her body. She knows where she is, but doesn't. She sees the blurry outline of her feet treading the creamy white slabs, feels the smack of a rubbish bin against her calf.

Things are all around her, below her and above her. A buzzing flying machine and the flap flap flap of canvas.

She looks up. A white banner spikes her eyes. THE VISUAL ARTS FESTIVAL WELCOMES THE WORLD'S GREATEST PORTRAITIST. Fiona can't make out the words. But she can the picture.

A fat man. With many chins. With shiny wee eyes and sparse eyebrows. A fat man with a fat nose and a fat wedge of a smile.

Sylvester does not know why Fiona suddenly freaked. Why she scuttled like a hysterical crab from side to side through the crush of pedestrians. Awful. Horrible.

Some of the pedestrians applauded. Some threw coins. Sylvester could see they thought she was a busker, a young drama student showing off. Because Fiona's behaviour, her crazy suffering, was too unreal to be real. Sylvester could see everyone wanted it to be make-believe.

When he finally managed to grab Fiona, drag her into the pub, get her away, he was shaking with rage and a deep helpless sorrow. It really was too much.

Now he pours drink down his friend, desperate to calm her.

'Is she OK?' asks the landlord. 'I don't want any trouble.'

Fiona turned eighteen in the spring. She celebrated her coming of age by riding the bus to her parents' home. She sang on the bus. She can't remember what she sang. She can't remember the toddlers who sat opposite her and watched wide mouthed and quiet as she sang. She can't remember the driver telling her to hush, or saying 'Aye, fuck off to you too,' as she swung from the bus. She can't remember toppling down the stairs to bang her head against her parents' front door, or smiling at the new neon sign which hangs in their salon window – MCLEOD'S FABULOUS HAIR. And she can't remember her father with his pinched startled face telling her to leave, to grow up, to sober up, to stop causing grief.

Fiona can't remember.

She drinks not to remember, and Sylvester knows this. He watched his mother do the same.

'Chicken and chips,' says Sylvester. He places the small oval basket before Fiona, hands her a knife and fork rolled in a paper serviette.

'Than',' says Fiona. Slowly she unravels the cutlery. She finds her fork, jabs it at a hazy object on the table. She knocks over the salt cellar.

Sylvester scoops the mess into his hands and throws the salt over his shoulder. 'Do you want me to cut it for you?' he asks.

He slides his knife through the chicken breast. His age-old wristwatch clinks against the pub table and the sound reminds Fiona of the bottle-cap sounds, glass sounds, money sounds she hears whilst curled in her hole.

Sylvester runs a slice of chicken across Fiona's lips. Her tongue responds, licking the fiery crinkled skin, the white flesh beneath. Sylvester feels pleased with himself. Fiona shows no signs of hysteria, no signs of her earlier panic. He believes she is coming round.

'You know,' he says, 'I'm enjoying this. We should do it more often. It's nice and normal. It's good.'

The chicken catches the back of Fiona's throat. It seems to sit there on purpose. She rubs her neck, trying to push the meat down. It is painful and prompting. She can feel her mind begin to shuffle its cards, trying to locate this memory. It starts with her clothes.

The cotton skirt her mother made her wear that first week at primary school. A yellow skirt with an elasticated waist. The skirt's hem edged with ricrac.

'No,' she shouts, fearful of what will come next. 'No.'

'Sorry,' apologizes Sylvester. He glances around the pub. People are looking. 'Sorry,' he nods at those closest. 'Sorry.' He bends to pick up the piece of chicken which shot from Fiona's mouth as she screamed. He returns it to her basket, and sighs to see her downing her drink in one.

Fiona sits slumped against Sylvester as they travel back to the docks. They ride the top deck of a city bus. Sylvester has the window seat, because windows offer nothing to Fiona. He watches the sights pass, feeling Fiona's skinny body warm by his side.

Last year Sylvester turned thirty. His life then was made up of signing on, drifting to and from the post office, the local shops, exchanging brief words with neighbours, watching the television, resisting the call of drink, drugs, and fist fights. It was an empty life which needed something.

Occasionally Sylvester thought a job would bring shape and order and meaning. But there are few jobs available in Sylvester's neighbourhood. Besides, he has never known what he could be employed as, or how to become employed.

He was feeling hopeless, until he spied Fiona from his living-room window. It was a frosty morning. The docks shimmered and a pearly pink winter sun outlined the girl as she inched across the concrete. Sylvester watched her young and angular body crawling into her hole. He saw her and recognized what made her, and suddenly felt purposeful, excited; he had an ambition.

But now the future he imagined for himself is beginning to pale. Some days he can't see it happening. Some days he is convinced Fiona's too far gone, too old in the head, too damaged. Some days he thinks he has made a big mistake.

'Mmm,' Fiona moans, as the bus speeds down the long road skirting the docks. The long, long road which she doesn't see any more, doesn't register any more. She is well gone, drunker than drunk.

Her mind is wild with images. It's running the film of her life, but there is no chronology, the time sequence has gone. The men from last night, all the men who've visited her hole, Sylvester, her mother and father, and the one who started it.

Fiona's mind is wild with images and she doesn't realize. Her body is responding and she doesn't realize. Her head is falling towards Sylvester's lap, her mouth making wide open shapes, nuzzling and searching.

Sylvester starts. 'Fiona!' he says. His hands reach for the girl, but her purpose is programmed, it is needy and urgent. Sylvester, his hands, cannot prevent it.

Sylvester steps off the bus with Fiona draped over his shoulders. She feels too light, too fragile. A shadowy person. A ghost. He glances at the summery sky as he heads for the docks and wishes it didn't look so cheerful, so unclouded and bright.

He crawls beneath the broken security fence and drags Fiona after him. He pulls her arms and she winces. He looks away from her hurt.

He didn't expect it of her, he did not expect her to do that to him and he didn't expect to respond the way he did. Sylvester slumped in his seat. He couldn't look at her; he pressed his face against the bus window. His hands flapped mildly. He came before Fiona unbuttoned his flies.

And still his groin aches with the dreadful warmth, the frightening sensation. It makes him move awkwardly as he props Fiona by her alcove.

The girl's head lolls, her tufts of hair catch the sun. Sylvester leans into her hole to tidy it. He flattens the remnant of carpet which he gave her last December. His Christmas present. A demonstration of his decent intentions. Sadly, he pads the blue and grey nylon pile with his hands, retracts when his fingers touch something wet and sticky.

'God Fiona,' he says. He looks at the girl, but she doesn't respond. Her body is limp, her energy used.

61

Sylvester's mother used to try to fix him up. She wanted her son to meet a nice girl, one with clean habits, who would care for him and give him love, proper love.

When drunk she accosted women in the street. She'd tug on their arms, grab their hands. She liked pretty girls, with fresh faces. She liked thin girls who wore neat jackets and pencil skirts. Jittery with fright they would break from her, scoot down the road dropping their bags of groceries, their little black handbags as they did so.

When sober Sylvester's mother wrote to dating agencies and pen pal clubs.

But Sylvester couldn't romance, not with his mother around. Besides, he felt a fraud. He believed he didn't have anything to offer an ordinary girl. And – though Sylvester doesn't want to – he still feels this way.

If Fiona could, if she had the guts, she'd stick a knife in herself, get it over and done with. She'd jump from a bridge into the city's river. She'd dowse herself with petrol and lay a match on her leg. She'd throw herself on the underground tracks, wait for a train to do its damage. She'd climb to the top of the ancient shipping crane and then dive, dive, dive.

Sylvester cleans his teeth. He watches himself in his bathroom mirror. Toothpaste bubbles from his mouth to disguise his lips. He tries to concentrate on its whiteness, to empty his mind. But still he thinks of Fiona.

It is late and he is tired. He should be in his bed. But everything moves slowly for him tonight, because of the girl, her persistent image, her stubbled hair and bruised young face. He rinses his toothbrush, shakes off the wet, hoping the motion will rid him of her. It cannot. He leaves his reflection. Nothing will.

He enters his living room and parts the flowery curtains. He wipes the condensation off the pane. It is beautiful outside.

The docks shine bright. A creamy moon spreads its translucent rays over the bleak concrete basins. A small black cat jumps the dockyard wall.

Sylvester concentrates on the animal's tail, its swishing, elegant movements. Then he looks towards the hole, and Fiona is there. He can see her feet, her tiny black pumps pointing upwards.

When Sylvester was small his mother used to hold his hands. Even indoors. She used to drag him from room to room by his hands. And Sylvester never protested, never complained as his mother led him into her secrets: the tiny boxroom jammed with bottles and cartons, smelling of damp and drink; the toilet with its brown stained bowl on which his mother would squat – her dress raised high, her legs mottled and lumpy.

When Sylvester grew bigger his mother let go of his hands, she let go of him, left him to wander, to find his own way. When lucid she would say it was for the best, that she couldn't hold his hands for ever; him relying on her, her relying on him.

Sylvester loved his mother. He loves her still.

He sat in the ambulance as she was sped to hospital. He held her hands then and she didn't resist. It felt good to touch her, to feel connected again to the one he knew, he understood most.

But it was scary too.

He felt the crazy pulse in her wrists, her chewed and horrible nails, the hard skin on her knuckles. She was a mess. Her cold palms drew heat from his. She was draining him, making him less.

Sylvester pulls Fiona from her hole. She murmurs, but doesn't wake. Her eyelids blank the world. Her mouth is open and her breath escapes sounding long and rested.

Sylvester is surprised by her calmness. He looks at her and she appears like a child, very young, sleeping a comfortable, loving night.

He cradles her in his arms and walks past the largest basin to the broken security fence. Fiona pushes her head against his chest. And though Sylvester knows this isn't really her, this is Fiona having a good moment, he feels a little hopeful, that he's doing right.

The sky is black now. The moon has gone behind a cloud. It is almost twelve. And Sylvester is taking Fiona to his home, to look after her properly.

Fiona's parents tried to care for her when she first fell sick. They tried to understand, to sympathize, to help their daughter out. But they found it hard, rescuing someone whilst running their business, living their lives. And she wasn't their baby. Not any more. She wasn't polite, she didn't smile. Six months of it was all they could take. Then they gave her some money, a rucksack for her clothes, but they refused to feel bad. Because Fiona's psychiatrist told them it wasn't their fault, that a choice is often involved, sacrifice, you or them.

Sylvester lays Fiona by the security fence. A car passes. Its headlamps glance the girl's body, Sylvester as he plucks at the netting. Sylvester's heart momentarily races, then it settles as the dark returns, the comforting black. His breathing matches Fiona's now. It is calm, certain, assured. He lifts the wire fence.

The metal makes a brittle chinking noise, which echoes in the air. A gentle sound that skips across the wasteland, dances round and down the dry wrecked basins, as Sylvester carries Fiona across the road, carries her into his tenement and over the threshold of his flat.

Better than Beer and Skittles

Frank drops me outside the sisters' flat. He waves goodbye in that leather-clad way of his before accelerating down the road. I watch a while, seeing how his bike's suspension copes with the pot holes and cracking tarmac. Then I remove my helmet and shake my hair, which is a silly move because I've very little hair to shake.

I had it cut a couple of days ago by my brother's girlfriend Geena. She smokes as she cuts and I half expected the singed look, but she's done a good job. She's clipped the back, but kept the fringe long. This is fine by me. I have this habit of pushing my fringe off my face when I talk, so I would miss it if it got the chop.

'You doing that so I can read your lips?' Frank has asked.

I try not to take offence: I know I have a quiet voice and the sisters turn their hearing aids up a notch when I visit. But I don't like his sarcasm. He can be cruel. Especially when we don't see eye to eye. Like now.

It's all to do with my visits here. Every Tuesday night I come, regular as clockwork, and at first he accepted it. But then the works' beer and skittles was moved to a Tuesday, and he wants me to go along.

But I won't. I won't give up the sisters' to spend an evening with the people I slave next to during the day. It's hard enough as it is to last my forty hours cooped up with Marjorie and Sheila and the rest packing those sausage rolls, six rolls to a box, every roll three inch by one inch, every box red and orange striped 'Authentic English Pork'.

(I dream of sausage rolls. I dream Marjorie and Sheila and the rest push the rolls one after the other down my throat until

I gag and balloon and finally burst – my insides, my brain, my heart, nothing but sausage roll.)

Frank won't listen. He says I'm too sensitive and swears he'll run off with Louise, the mini-skirted dwarf from Quality Control. But I know he won't. We have something, Frank and I. When we're on together, it's fireworks. Yes.

'Hello, love,' says Helen, tapping me on the shoulder as I stroll up the entry.

'Hiya,' I say. 'Are you alone?'

'Oh no,' sighs Helen. 'He's out there again. I've pleaded with him, but he says he's doing no harm; just checking his wife's up to nothing immoral.'

'Immoral,' I say. 'Big word.' I look past Helen's shoulder and can just make out the front end of a blue Fiesta. Inside sits Derek, her husband, a fat man with no taste. He wears bright orange and red lumberjack shirts, shiny tracksuit bottoms and shoes with Cuban heels. He's about fifty and believes the sisters' is a knocking shop.

Ever since Helen's first visit six months ago he's parked his car and, fingers drumming against the dashboard, has waited to catch her at it. A diseased mind. He must know by now only women visit the sisters'. Perhaps he thinks we're porno dykes, imagines our sewing boxes hide kinky sex aids. I doubt it though. He's missionary position man. I can tell. Sex for him is the dainty woman lying back and thinking of England, the bulldog pumping her from above. Do I sound bitter? Mmm, well I've had my share of Dereks, before I met Frank. Frank and his fabulous foreplay.

'Rose phoned the other day,' says Helen, slipping the key in the sisters' front-door lock. 'Asked me to bring some Fisherman's Friends. Apparently Ivy has a summer cold. She's been in bed all week.'

'Got to be careful at her age,' I say, pushing open the door. We step into the flat. I love this flat. The sisters haven't changed a thing for years. The wallpaper is old, creamy and covered in pink flowers. The carpets are worn thin and have lost their colour. Everywhere smells fusty, like the inside of my nephew's duffel bag; the one he uses for PE.

Rose comes out of the Quilting Room to greet us. 'Did you manage to get the Fisherman's Friends?' she asks. Helen nods and fumbles in her skirt pocket.

'For fuck's sake,' shouts Jean, her voice husky from fags, reaching us from the room. 'Grab her before she collapses. Eighty-eight is not the age to go chasing Fisherman's Friends.'

'I've always liked a sailor,' jokes Rose. She's wearing her green dress again, which suits her. It is very low at the front and shows her cleavage and small breasts. She always dangles a necklace between her breasts. Today it's her fruit and nut necklace, made from varnished hazelnuts and wood cut to look like a slice of pear or peach or apple. She must have been a real goer when young. Don't know why she never married, probably had more sense.

I follow Rose and Helen into the Quilting Room. Jean gives us a queenly wave of welcome, whilst Ivy smiles. Two years older than Rose, Ivy looks like she's at death's door. Her hair is very white, though she wears it down in a girlie way, with clips holding it from her eyes. Jean bought her the clips for her last birthday. One is a luminous orange that glows in the dark, the other is pink with gold glitter sprinkled on it. She also has a lime-green headband which is dotted with huge cream daisies, but she only wears this when she feels like partying. The horrible thing about Ivy is her skin. It is very wrinkled and covered in large brown blotches. It hangs off her like she's lost a lot of weight. Poor Ivy. She looks flushed. It must be her cold, or perhaps it's the sunlight shining through the window. It glows around her head like a halo.

'Come and sit down,' says Jean, sewing to the left of Ivy.

Jean is the one who got me into this. She's a funny woman:

67

funny ha ha and funny peculiar. She gets obsessions.

She was first married to Lyle, still alive, a good-looking bloke who runs the local pop round. Jean talks of him fondly. 'The first you marry for love, the second for money,' she says. Lyle was a real love. When Jean gets on the vodkas and limes she tells of how Lyle made her heart beat. She remembers hot, exciting nights. Lyle is no missionary position man. He's inventive. But Jean is into status. She couldn't live for long with a man whose sole income comes from selling lemonade. So she ran off with George.

George is the opposite of Lyle. He's short for a start, but he's also rich. He owns a chain of discount stores; those shops where you can get sanitary towels made from shredded cardboard for 20p a dozen. The type of shop that is doing our Ozone. His hairsprays are lethal. Geena uses them on the blue-rinse OAPs, those that like their hair to be as stiff as a corpse.

But George is not all bad. He bought Jean her patchwork and quilting shop; something she'd been hankering after for ages. She loves her business. She claims that patchwork is an important art form, that it speaks volumes about women. She goes on about this, strutting around her shop like the original burn your bra. Silly cow. I tell Jean she's not liberated, she's owned by George. But she won't have it. 'I chose him,' she says. 'I'm in control.'

And that was how I first met her, doing her I'm in control bit, when I went to Mother Goose to buy some cottons. She seized me by the shoulders and pointed out a notice.

'Help!' it said, in scrawly spider hand. 'We are two ancient ladies trying to achieve the impossible. Fifteen years ago we set ourselves the task of sewing quilts for all our nephews and nieces. We have managed to sew a quilt a year so far, but we still have four quilts to go. As our eyesight and everything else is failing we would appreciate a hand with these remaining quilts. Once a week will do. Tuesdays at 7.00 p.m. Come to Lower Flat, 20 Kennedar Drive. Tea and biscuits served. Mind next-door's Alsatian.'

'I think,' said Jean, 'we ought to attend this, you and I. I can see you're the type who's looking for something extra. Be a change, get you away from chasing the men, hey?'

Frank told me to steer clear, but there's something about Jean which is very persuasive. She has this face that dares you. She's pulling it now, because I'm refusing to settle.

It takes me a while to start my sewing. I like to wander, to look at my friends, to chat. I'm like a bee droning every place but on the flower where I should be, sucking up my honey.

'Samantha, you got ants in your pants?' says Jean.

'She's just admiring the decor,' smiles Ivy, who knows the way I go about things.

'It's nice,' I say. 'I know what to expect when I come here.'

'A tip,' chuckles Rose, passing the packet of Fisherman's Friends to her elder sister.

Ivy opens the packet. She picks a sweet and drops it in her skinny mouth. 'Yuk,' she says.

When Jean and I first visited the sisters' we had a bit of a shock. They are not your normal everyday old ladies; not at all like Granny stuck as she is in the past with nothing in her head but death. No, Rose and Ivy have spunk, ambition. They began their quilting marathon when Rose turned seventy, Ivy seventy-two. They pooled their savings to buy a huge quilting frame, which they assembled from a kit in their living room, now called the Quilting Room. In their hurry, they didn't clear the room to make proper space for the frame, but pushed every piece of furniture outwards. Even now their sofa, telly, radio, bookcase, drinks bar and aquarium line the walls of the room like they are second-hand goods awaiting the rag and bone man.

The aquarium is best. It stands on the sofa and the fish swim back and forth against a backdrop of cream and brown stripes. Jean, when she first saw this, thought of contacting the sea-creatures' branch of the RSPCA, but changed her mind. The fish look healthy. There are always six of them and they always shine golden, not white like they are sickening. OAP fishes. Perhaps they live off the dust which hangs like curtains in this topsy-turvy room.

'The Twilight Zone,' says Frank when I talk about it. 'Strange things happen to those who enter the Twilight Zone. Little old ladies turn into willy-weirdo witches. Watch out. They'll strap you to their frame one of these days, and will suck away your youth and beauty.'

Beauty! I often tell Frank he should write, such a vivid imagination he's got. But he says he has no time, that he's devoted to becoming a world-class beer and skittles man. Could be Jean's right: 'The first you marry for love, the second for money.'

Today Jean is dressed in her Spanish costa packet outfit. A bolero trouser suit made of red felt-like fabric and fringed with black tassels. She looks a bugger, but somehow carries it off. Confidence, I suppose. Helen, who has taken my place beside Jean, is a different kind of woman. She's into catalogue twinsets. Make her look kind of dowdy, but no doubt her husband wouldn't want her to dress in anything more appealing.

Helen joined us ladies off her own bat. She heard about Ivy and Rose through the neighbourhood grapevine. She loves sewing, wanted to be a needlework teacher once, and so defied her husband for the very first time and came here. She reminds Ivy of her and Rose's mother: a small sweet person who was married to a drayman. His first love was beer, the second horses. Women weren't noticed until they didn't get the dinner on time. Same with Helen's husband. He didn't take much notice of her until she started trekking out on Tuesday nights. Then he began to play the Grand Old Man Possessive. Sometimes Helen mentions how she makes him a treat steak and kidney to butter him up, mostly though she keeps her mouth shut. She pushes him to one side like he's a nasty mess that needs seeing to, but not before she has had her fun.

Her sewing box is neat and tidy, a real tool of pleasure. The quilting cottons are arranged by colour; the needles stuck in straight lines in the padded lid of the box; her thimble, which she slips on her finger now, having a special resting place wrapped in a lace hanky. 'Touch the quilt, Samantha,' says Helen to me, looking at it like a lover.

'Beautiful,' I say, running my hand, which I've checked to see is clean, over the ivory and cream silk and the teeny-weeny quilting stitches. The quilt is the sisters' last, their nineteenth. It's for their great-great-great-niece who is ten years old. All the quilts that the sisters have sewn take away the breath, but this one can't be beat.

Ivy and Rose have quilted from the year dot. They made quilts for their mother from scraps. The quilts were usually used for bedding, though Ivy has told us how her mother once persuaded their landlord to take a crazy quilt in exchange for a fortnight's rent. Jean thinks this is a wonderful story and has added it to the patchwork exhibition she's set up in the room above her shop. She got Ivy to write the story out, and has stuck it with a picture of a crazy quilt on a display board under the heading: 'Quilts vs homelessness. Women do it again!' A lovely image, but I bet many landlords, even in the old days, would sooner have had a bit of the other. I know my landlord, when I'm behind with the readies, wants payment with some up and under. But I'm not having it: once they're in your pants, they're hard to get out. Got to be careful in this twentieth century. One man, a heavy-duty rubber and a closed back passage.

'This seat taken?' I ask Rose, plonking myself down on the only free chair in the room. A wonky chair, it rocks in time to your sewing arm.

'It's yours, no strings,' says Rose, smiling.

'Why thanks.' I rest my sewing box on my knee. I click it open and rummage through my jumble of cottons and pins and needles and templates. 'Do you think this is going to wash all right?' I ask.

'The quilt?' says Helen.

'Mmm.' I find a decent needle and thread it through my jumper so I can't lose it.

'Don't see why not,' says Jean.

'Well those dresses were never meant for washing. You're only supposed to wear them once.'

'Nothing to worry about. I washed them when we got them home and they were fine,' says Ivy, looking as if she couldn't wash a pair of pants, let alone four wedding dresses. 'We always do this for every quilt. You should know, Samantha.'

'Sorry,' I say, flushing. I don't know where I'm coming from today. It must be Frank. He's upsetting me more than I thought. Because I do know the sisters are very thorough about their quilts and would never make one which couldn't be cleaned or spun, which would shrink or fall apart. They don't cut corners. They make their quilts just how their mother taught them to when they were small.

So they never buy new fabrics. They use old fabrics, like second-hand clothes or curtains. They unpick them, wash them, discard the pieces which shrivel or lose colour. Then they iron the material, play around with it, matching this and that, before cutting it up, before sewing. Making something new and different from something else.

The sisters say that by reusing fabrics they add a little extra to the quilts. I agree. I watched a programme once where this woman, whose daughter had died, made a quilt from the daughter's summer dresses, so when she slept beneath the quilt she felt her daughter was still alive in some way, close to her. 'Spooky,' said Frank, bullied into watching. 'Too arty-farty for her own good.' But Frank has no idea: he can't get his head round this nineteenth quilt at all, made as it is from wedding dresses.

Jean helped the sisters get the dresses. She took them out to Bridal Delight, which is on the verge of bankruptcy – too many youngsters living in the big S for Sin – and they bought them at the cheapest of prices. The sisters chose wedding dresses because they want this quilt to say something about being pure. I say a wedding dress in this modern world is more than a sure sign the bride's been tried and tested. Used goods, but clean used goods – if you get my drift – is all that's wanted now. A disease-free bride. But Rose and Ivy won't have it. They believe their dresses speak of innocent things, like the Virgin Mary; like their old age without sex; like their little niece who is still before sex.

Frank tells me this last part is crap, loads of his friends reckon they know ten-year-olds who are dying for it. I say it's wishful thinking. Men like to imagine there are nympho ten-year-olds walking the streets, when really little girls have nothing more on their minds than hamburgers and soap stars. Perhaps when they reach twelve it's different. Twelve is when your breasts begin to show. Twelve is when John across the road touched me up in his den. My first.

I take my quilting needle from my jumper. I hold it high so the summer sunlight shines through the eye, making it easier for me to know exactly where to stick my cotton, and I thread it. The funny thing about John, he's only supposed to have one ball, that's what Louise, the mini-skirted dwarf from Quality Control tells me, but I can't remember.

'Day-dreamer, wake up!' says Jean. She gives me a look with her hard face, before bending over the quilt again, her black backcombed hair making an ugly spider shadow upon the silk. Perhaps I ought to introduce her to Geena and her magic scissors, but then Jean's hair is like Buckingham Palace, a national monument. It would go against God, England and the Tories to touch it.

I sew a stitch. 'Are you watching, Jean?' I ask.

'And about time too.' She smiles, not one to hold a grudge for long. 'We've got a lot to do on this.'

Too true. The quilt is just a plain strip quilt which suits the silk, but it's covered in real difficult stitching. This is something new. Ivy and Rose usually go for a tidy running stitch which follows the outline of the patchwork shapes such as 'Shoo-Fly' or 'The Grandmother's Fan'. But for this quilt they have pricked out a design of 'Cable' and 'Feather Wreath'. It's not quite like embroidering the whole quilt, but it's close. Time consuming. We've been at it for nine months. The sisters joke they've made this last piece so fiddly to delay things. They're afraid, as we all are, about what's going to happen once this last quilt is sewn.

Jean has pressed the sisters to hold an exhibition of all nineteen quilts, once the nineteenth is finished, in her shop. A good idea for her business, certainly draw in the crowds, but, as she admitted to Helen on the quiet, it would give the sisters something to look forward to. The sisters said no. They're unsure if all nephews and nieces have kept their quilts, whether all would be returned, whether they'd look as clean and as good as when they were made. They told Jean they'd be upset to see tea stains or egg stains or sick or sex upon their handiwork. So they turned down the offer, as usual not mincing their words.

'You're beginning to fill out, Samantha,' says Rose, stitching expertly and fast, proving my point.

'Tell me about it,' I mutter. Frank has been saying the same thing, says my breasts are getting heavier and my belly more rounded. He wants a kid so he's hoping that's the reason. I'm hoping it's age creeping on. Once you hit twenty-five they do say the body goes. I don't want my body to go, but I'd sooner that than a kiddy. I can't face the thought of squeezing one out: the pain. I don't like pain. And what happens when it gets to be a teenager? Teenagers treat mothers like shit. I threw a can of tomato soup at mine when she wouldn't allow me at fifteen to go to the Free and Easy Singles Disco down Canal Street. It hit her on the thigh. I was aiming for her heart.

'Oh, but I think it suits you,' says Ivy. 'Bonny. You can be too thin, you know.' She snuffles and rummages in her pocket for a Fisherman's Friend.

'Thinness equals meanness of spirit. Look at me!' laughs Rose.

'Your spirit is far from mean,' says Helen quietly.

But I can't be bothered with this, I'm rattled. 'Well, I'm not pregnant if that's what you're getting at,' I nip. 'Precaution is the name of the game with me.' I stitch the curve of a Cable badly and, tutting, begin to unpick the thread.

'There's nothing wrong with being pregnant,' says Jean. She's speaking with her head bent more so over the quilt. 'I loved it.'

'You pregnant!' What a revelation. I thought Jean was the original Ms Contraception. I stop my sewing.

'Mmm,' says Jean. 'Didn't last long. Lyle got me humping round his crates of pop. I lost it. Just sat down on the toilet and there it went. Whoosh. Like a big period.'

'But that's awful,' I say. Jean has never opened up like this before. Usually she is jokey or all strident new woman. Perhaps I should hug her or something, but she doesn't look huggable in that bullfighter's outfit. I can see Helen and Rose and Ivy are thinking the same. So awkward. Ivy is losing herself in her hanky, whilst Rose touches her necklace like she has prayer beads in her hands. Helen just looks shocked, doubly shocked, because suddenly there he is pressing his outsized nose against the window pane.

'I know you're in there,' shouts Helen's husband. 'I know what you're doing. You bitch. Has he got it up you yet? You're breaking my heart.' He raises a hand to shade his eyes, trying to see into the room.

Jean is first off the mark. She helps Ivy from her chair. 'Better move back, just in case,' she says.

'Yes,' I whisper, watching the orange and red lumberjack shirt as it sways backwards, forwards. It blocks out the usual view of the sisters' flower boxes, stray dogs, kids and council flats. I begin to wish next-door's Alsatian, which used to cause us so much trouble, hadn't died. It would've sunk its teeth into Derek for sure.

'Getting enough are you? Enjoying yourself?' the bully shouts. 'I can see you. I can see you.' He bangs his fists hard against the glass. Thump. Thump. Thump. Thump. Bloody big fists, like flesh-covered boxing gloves. I wonder whether he uses them on Helen: she's never actually said.

'I'll go out to him,' she murmurs. She looks afraid, shrunk into her acrylic twinset.

'No don't,' says Rose. 'That's what he's wanting.'

'Too right,' says Jean, stepping up to the window.

'For fuck's sake,' I say, pushing my fringe off my face. Old habits die hard even in troubled times. 'What are you playing at?'

Jean flaps a hand. 'I'm going to teach this bastard a lesson.'

She pulls back her bolero jacket to undo the blouse beneath. One by one the buttons slip from their holes. Easy. 'George likes this outfit,' she smiles. 'It's husband friendly.'

Ivy, Rose, Helen and me: we are quiet. Can't say a word. There is Jean and she looks magnificent. The blouse has fallen open and there shines her body – brown, healthy and perfect. Her breasts are much better than mine. They are big, motherly, but they don't sag. They are powerful. A black tassel fringing her bolero rests just above the left nipple. It's a finishing touch. She looks like a painting hung on the wrong wall, because all the while, behind her, stands this pathetic angry man.

Jean turns to face him. 'Watch my technique, girls,' she says. She begins to rub herself against the pane, up and down, up and down. I can only see her back, but it's enough for me. I squeal, excited: my head full of lovely tits pressing fat and warm upon the icy glass.

'Ooohh,' I squeal. 'Ooohh.'

'Sshh, Samantha, sshh,' whispers Helen, her eyes brighter, no longer frightened. 'You'll spoil her concentration.'

'You know,' says Rose, huddling up. 'That kind of wiggle takes years of practice. I myself have never mastered the art.'

'Monroe,' says Ivy. 'She had it.'

'Oh quiet,' says Helen. 'Jean's having problems, can't you see? I reckon Derek needs glasses.'

And true, it looks like Jean's show is wasted. Helen's husband peers through the window, blind as a bat to her gorgeous flesh. Till she stretches up, pretending to kiss him. Then it registers, and it's like he's witnessed death. His face turns a ghastly white and he begins to back from the window, his arms held out, sweat patches darkening his lumberjack shirt. 'That's it, boy,' shouts Jean, triumphant. 'You've no idea, have you?' She works her body wilder now, like an upmarket belly dancer.

'Never,' says Ivy. 'Have I seen anything so . . . '

'Marvellous,' laughs Rose. 'And look at Derek. What a Derek! He's been hit between the eyes!'

'Enough,' shouts Jean. She spins round and with a final nifty move draws the Quilting Room curtains on the man.

'Wonderful,' I say. 'Bloody wonderful.' I imagine Derek stumbling to his Fiesta, see him tripping over his own feet – so confused is he, so winded.

I reach for the lamp, which stands on top of the sisters' drinks bar, and I switch it on. The lamp has an orange glass shade and the light shining through it makes the room glow magical. The quilt shimmers. The water in the aquarium appears a dark blue like the deepest blue of the sea where whales and stingrays swim. I feel very safe, and I can see that Helen and Rose and Ivy and Jean, who has buttoned her blouse, feel very safe too. There's a Famous Five feeling. Yes.

'I believe there are a few old bottles of rum and gin and perhaps sherry in that bar,' says Rose.

'And glasses,' adds Ivy. 'Nice ones too. If I remember rightly they have a pattern of gold crisscrosses around the brims.'

'I could do with a drink,' admits Helen. 'Make mine a large one.'

*

I sit with Rose and Ivy and Helen and Jean around the quilting frame. We slug our booze, making sure not a drop spills upon the quilt, but going for it all the same. 'You know,' I say. 'Frank's been trying to get me to jack this in. Wants me to go to the works' beer and skittles night instead.'

'But this is much better than beer and skittles,' says Ivy, poking around in her Fisherman's Friends' packet for another sweet.

'I know,' I smile. 'And what's more I don't think you should be mixing cough stuff with the strong stuff.'

'You tell her,' laughs Jean, trying to run her hand through her black backcombed hair, but getting her fingers stuck halfway.

Family Fears

I'm on the number 3 bus travelling from Five Oaks to Rozel. It is hot. The sun glares through the window. Sweat trickles from my armpits. I wipe the palms of my sticky hands on my shorts.

I'd like to move to a shadier spot, but the bus is packed. There's a queue of people standing in the gangway, all seats are occupied.

It's an unhappy bus load. Nobody smiles. Fathers whack their kids for whining. Mothers grimace. The two women in front argue bitterly. I clutch my stomach, made nauseous by pregnancy.

Rob sits next to me. He's pretending to be somewhere else. He gazes, blank-eyed, at the roof of the bus. He does not seem to notice my discomfort, and occasionally adds to it, moving his elbow to jab me in the side. I choose not to point this out. I don't want to get into one of our futile talks which go round and round in circles. I'm fed up with them. They exhaust me. Everything exhausts me.

I am eleven weeks pregnant. And from the day I conceived – though I had no idea I'd conceived – I've felt terrible. When I visited the doctor's I cried, believing I had a fatal disease. He told me I was creating a new life and that such work wouldn't come easy. He told me I'd get a break in the middle three months. The honeymoon period. I long for this time. I need space from the physical symptoms to think, and to reason with Rob.

The bus turns a sharp corner, narrowly missing a stone wall.

'Whoa . . . ' cry the people in the aisle as they fall against each other. I smile, and look to see if Rob smiles too, but he continues to stare at the roof. He's as stubborn as the two women in front who, despite the commotion, still bicker.

The women are sisters. There's no mistaking it. They dress differently, but their profiles are the same. They have hooked nose profiles, pointed chins, smallish foreheads, beady ferret-like eyes. They are sisters, but they behave like enemies. They scold and nip. They raise their hands, edging to slap.

Rob has three sisters. He has a photograph of them in his flat. They sit arm in arm on a flowery sofa. They look relaxed with each other and happy. Rob loves his sisters. He loves his mum and dad. He kisses them hello. He kisses them goodbye. He shares everything with them. Already he has sent them postcards of Jersey Zoo, Grosnez Point and Rozel Harbour.

Rozel Harbour is one of the quieter bays in Jersey. The beach is stony which discourages many people, especially those who want to build sand castles. But I like it. I like it because it is quiet and because it is charming. Small boats sit waiting for the tide to come in. Ducks and geese mingle with the seagulls, taking turns to float on the ocean, to march along the pebbles, to bathe in the warm water spilling from the hotel overflow. There is only the one hotel, a discreet stone affair. Next to it runs the causeway, and beyond the causeway a small row of wooden shanty shops and cafés. We have been on holiday for a week, and for three days out of this week we have visited Rozel.

The bus backs into its lay-by and the driver signals for people to get off. The mothers and fathers and kids make their noisy way to the nearby pub. It is dinnertime. Everybody is hungry and thirsty. I point to the pub, but Rob shakes his head. He lifts my shopping bag on to his shoulder and makes down the road to the beach. I follow him, hating my acquiescence.

We enter a small café on the sea front. Rob digs his hand into his trouser pocket, removes his wallet. I stand by his side, determined not to say the first word. He looks at me. 'What do you want?' he asks.

I smile. 'An orange juice, please.'

The woman behind the counter pours the juice. She wears a

striped dress made out of stretch cotton. It clings to her big bones. She strikes me as sexy and I am jealous. I want to be that free with my body, to flaunt my flesh. Like I used to, before the baby took over.

My friends ask me why I'm keeping this baby, because I seem to resent it so. I tell them I'm keeping the baby because I can't imagine getting rid of it. I tell them a story about a girl I met at college who'd had an abortion at fifteen and still seven years later was lighting candles for the foetus, praying for forgiveness. I tell them I'm a coward and I'm mixed up.

I take the juice and move to a table, tucked into the far corner of the café. I want somewhere private, shaded. I want to be alone. Nausea still lines my throat. My stomach is shaken. And I feel defeated, my mind battered by Rob.

He paid for this holiday. When he waved the aeroplane tickets before me, he said, 'This is what we both need. Get us away from our jobs, get us away from the pressure. You'll see, a little bit of sun, a little bit of sand and things won't seem so bad.' I kissed him then. I believed he'd decided to give me what I most want – a break, a rest, some time. I strapped myself into the aeroplane seat, watched home slide away and felt so hopeful. But as soon as we got to the hotel, he started pestering me again.

We have been together for five years. Our relationship has been an unfettered one. He's lived on one side of town. I've lived on the other. It's suited me. It seemed to suit him. But now I'm pregnant and keeping the baby, he wants our lives to change. He wants me to live with him, to prepare a nest, to turn us into a family.

When I was fourteen Mum, Dad, my sister and I went to Spain. Our first holiday abroad. We stayed in a small white cottage, with terracotta roof tiles. The cottage was owned by a farmer. It sat on some coarse scrub. It had two bedrooms, a bathroom and a large kitchen and living room combined. The walls separating the rooms were made of a thin grey plasterboard. You could hear everything. You could hear how quiet we were, how we never really spoke. One day my sister and I broke out. We danced around the kitchen to a Spanish pop song blaring from the radio. We flung our arms about and laughed and shouted. 'Stop that,' said my mother and we did. We spent the rest of the holiday sitting with our parents outside the cottage. My mother crocheted. My father slept. My sister and I read magazines. It was just how we behaved at home, except it was worse, heightened by being alone in the middle of a field, in the middle of a foreign country.

I sip the juice, watch the people outside the café. A small boy, with a bucket and spade clutched in one hand, skips around the parked cars. The sisters from the bus wait for deckchairs. They flap at each other like agitated hens. Then the younger-looking one grabs the elder, pulls her arm roughly backwards and upwards into a half nelson.

'Did you see that?' I say to Rob, who plants himself opposite me.

'Not interested,' says Rob. He has bought himself a large bowl of multicoloured ice cream. Around the ice cream runs a trail of chocolate sauce. He takes a scoop and pushes it into his mouth. He's feeling combative. I can sense he's decided today is the day.

I drain the glass of juice, avoid looking at him, stare at the milk machine. I watch the machine's stainless steel arm whip the white cool milk. 'You're not being fair,' I say.

'I'm not being fair!' Rob moves his head in front of the milk machine, so I have to look at him. Around his mouth is a line of pink and green ice cream. Messy as a toddler.

'You've missed your mouth,' I say, pointing to his lips, but not touching his skin.

'God, Beth,' says Rob. He wipes a serviette over his face, smearing the ice cream into his hairline. 'Why are you avoiding it?'

'It's in your hair now,' I say.

'Then you have it,' says Rob. He pushes his bowl of melted ice cream towards me.

'It'll make me sick,' I say. I put my hands on the plastic café table, to lever myself out of my chair. 'Everything makes me sick.'

'Oh Beth,' says Rob. 'Please sit down. We have to talk.'

I stand up. 'I'm going for a walk,' I say. 'I need some fresh air.'

I leave the café, pass by the sisters who carry their deckchairs. The younger sister walks effortlessly, her muscled fist knotting her chair to her side. The elder sister struggles. She has tried to tuck her chair under her arm like a newspaper. But it's too heavy for her. It keeps slipping to drag along the road. I smile at her, and I think I hear her say 'It's not smiles I need.'

I head for the rocks lining the far side of the beach. The sun coats my shoulders, the back of my neck, as I walk down the causeway, tread the stony sand. I don't look behind me. I'm afraid Rob may be following. Pursuing me till he gets the response he wants.

I find a boulder, free from the slime of wet seaweed, and sit down. A seagull swoops to land close by. The sudden flap of wings startles me. I look up, register the bird's beaky face, its strange open eyes, somebody approaching. I expect Rob and brace myself.

The younger sister places her deckchair on the solid sand fronting my rock and kicks at the gull. 'Woo! Woo!' she shrieks. The gull rises into the air, hooting sharply. 'Nasty things,' she says.

She erects her chair, patting the stripy canvas with her hands. I watch her stocky body as it moves around the chair. She is dressed in a long-sleeved T-shirt, brown knitted leggings. Sweat shimmers on her face. She removes her shoulder bag and places it on the seat of her chair. 'Constance,' she shouts. 'Hurry up.'

Her elder sister picks her way through the sleeping sun-bathers. A middle-aged man in beige shorts carries her chair. He reminds me of Rob's father. Guileless. Kind. He wears a bemused smile and a floppy beach hat.

I once went for a drink with Rob's father. It was a cold wintry day. We sat huddled together on a bench in a local pub. I can't remember how we came to be there, alone. Rob probably arranged it, as he arranged my bowling trip with his sisters, my sauna with his mother. Rob wants me to get along with his family. And I do. I enjoyed sipping my beer, listening to his father tell his tales. It was like listening to a story on the radio, a story told in comforting tones about sleepy lives and endless good times. He told me about his childhood, just after the war, when he swam in the village pond using his sister's knickers for trunks. He told me about his mother's enormous bust, the way she tried to hide it under large shapeless aprons.

Then he wanted to know about my family and I had to say, 'There's nothing to tell, we went on holidays and we waited to come home.'

Rob's father thought I was joking. He winked at me, like Rob often winks at me. 'Oh come on now,' he said.

'Constance,' screeches the younger sister. 'Where did you put the suntan cream? Don't tell me you've forgotten to pack it? Constance!'

She stands over her sister's chair. I watch as she wraps her sturdy hands around the wooden frame. She tugs, but Constance digs her heels into the sand, nestles her bony bottom deep into the chair and refuses to answer. 'Constance,' screeches the younger sister. 'Constance!'

I feel sorry for these sisters. They fight over the smallest things. The younger sister pummels at Constance, her whole body desperate to knock through their differences. But Constance seems more resigned, disposed to sit it out. She reminds me of my parents, passively waiting.

*

Last summer I broke from my parents. I stopped visiting. I stopped phoning. I stopped wanting them to give me what they will never give. A little happiness. A sense of belonging. Warmth.

Last summer I broke from my sister, because she wouldn't understand. Because she was too wrapped up in them, willing them to care for each other, to come together, to hold each other and hold her too.

Last summer I felt released.

I turn from the sisters, try to concentrate on a speed boat breaking out of the harbour. A white speed boat with a flash of silver and the name 'Princess' painted on its prow. I imagine I see the French coastline and maybe I do. A green streak on the horizon. Enticing.

Rob laughed when I first told him I wanted to escape, to pack my bags and flee. He said his mother had felt the same through all her pregnancies. 'Hormonal,' he said. 'Natural.'

Then he stopped laughing. Because it's so obvious I'm not his mother. Because it's so obvious I'm frightened. 'But you can't avoid the family,' he argued. 'You're having a baby. A baby is family.'

The hotel gong sounds. Lunch is done. It alarms the ducks treading the hotel wall. It alarms me. The dull note threads through my nausea, makes my body stiffen, my legs swing. My legs are a reminder of my childless days. They are thin, free-looking. I envy them.

I watch a small group of people leave the hotel, walk through the gap in its wall on to the beach. I see Rob standing near the wall. His hands are raised, shielding his eyes from the sun. He searches for me.

I trace the outline of his body, witness his solid shape. He is not like me. I knew that when we first met. It wasn't important then.

*

He finds me and lifts his hand to wave. I wave back. Then signal for him to stay where he is. Him at one end of the beach, me at the other. With a fresh salty breeze blowing between us.

Party Piece

Lorraine sits on the top deck of the Clydeside 23 dressed as an alien. She wears blue washing-up gloves tied on a band round her head. She's painted her face blue. She's wrapped her body in blue Cellophane and has sprinkled it with glitter. On her feet are a pair of blue flip flops. She feels very hot and very stupid, but she's on her way to a party, a Fantasy Space Party.

This is the first time Lorraine's travelled on a Glasgow bus in fancy dress, and she realizes she's made a mistake. The other passengers blow kisses and stare at her Cellophane-covered breasts. Lorraine is wearing a swimsuit under the Cellophane, but their attention makes her feel naked. Down below the driver shouts 'Hold on to your panties ET!' as he zooms round a corner, pushing the bus into fourth.

Lorraine wishes she'd worn her summer mac to hide her outfit, wishes she'd taken a taxi, wishes she'd stayed in her flat. But as usual she has had a dreadful day. She arrived home from work exhausted, defeated, and wasn't thinking straight.

Lorraine is a box-office clerk. She works at the Theatre Victoria which stands in the centre of Glasgow. The theatre is a seedy building, painted dark brown. A canopy covers the six-doored entrance. The canopy is dull gold, THEATRE VICTORIA is sten-cilled on its billowing form. The stencil is peeling and reads THE TRE ORIA. Visitors to the city sometimes mistake it for an Italian restaurant. Especially the culture vultures. They don't expect this to be one of Glasgow's principal theatres: venue for classic and contemporary drama, for big-name actors and rising stars.

Lorraine used to act. At junior school she was the lid to

Pandora's box: she had to roll to one side as the box was opened and all the blessings escaped except Hope. Lorraine had wanted to be Hope, but the part was given to Sharon the only black girl in the school. Mr Chris the teacher-producer thought it would be a good idea to give Sharon a positive role, a sense of pride. He thought it would make her popular. He couldn't believe she had six best friends, was always being invited to parties and had never been picked on in the playground.

At thirteen Lorraine joined a drama group. It was fun. She discovered boys. She discovered that the best parts were given to boys and the good-looking girls. She was a good-looking girl. She played Snow White. She played Blanche. She played Jimmy Porter's wife in *Look Back In Anger*. Her drama teacher said she was talented and encouraged her to apply for drama school. Lorraine didn't get past the interview. The panel said she was no Helen Mirren. But her mother was kind. She took Lorraine to the doctors and asked for anti-depressants, then paid for Lorraine to study shorthand and typing, and later word processing.

Lorraine worked as a temp and went to the theatre at night. For years she still wanted to be part of it. At first she believed she would get to perform somehow, somewhere. Finally she settled for backstage. She wrote off to theatres in Glasgow, Edinburgh, Perth and Stirling. Only the Theatre Victoria replied.

Lorraine has been working in the Victoria's box office for as long as she's been living in Glasgow. In the beginning it thrilled her like the city. But now Glasgow has lost its shine and so has the job. She has come to realize that backstage is not Thespian. It is without glamour, and clerking is boring, badly paid and boring.

Lorraine waddles off the escalator which has brought her from the tube up to the breezy cosmopolitan air of Kelvinbridge. She has travelled halfway across Glasgow, from Govan to the city centre, from there to the West End. She feels exhausted and humiliated and keeps her head low as she shuffles from the station.

She blanks the *Big Issue* seller edging from foot to foot at the tube exit. She shies from the trendy couples, dressed in black jeans and white shirts, micro minis and skinny rib tops, who swing by discussing Japanese food, Pam Hogg's band, holidaying in South America.

Lorraine moved to Glasgow four years ago. She was fed up with England and the town she was living in, fed up with its insignificant streets, boring architecture, middling skies and yellow-green grass. She was ready for change, and as soon as she was offered the box-office job, she packed her bags, boarded the train.

It was exhilarating. She felt she was this close to adventure, this close to living. She felt the excitement of being a foreigner, and no chicken foreigner either, but a foreigner living deep in foreign territory. Living outside Glasgow's multicultural West End. Living in Govan. Closed off Govan, where everyone is related, where a strange face and a strange accent is noticed, remarked on, sometimes visited. A knock on the door. The second day. 'Are you alone, hen? Are you English?'

But she's lived here too long now. She no longer raises sweat as she passes the lads throwing stones at the off-licence shutters, the mothers and children as they gather in her street on a summer's day drinking their Tennent's, their Irn Bru. The women at the post office know her, the families in her close know her, and they smile and chat briefly, commenting on the weather. These little acceptances have spoilt it for Lorraine. They have erased the daring, diminished the suspense. They have nibbled at her spirit. And now her cellar flat seems too dank and lonely, her life too flimsy and sad.

Every morning she wakes depressed, feeling like someone has strapped her to her bed. She can barely lift her arms and legs, barely raise her head to glance at the curtains to see if sunlight plays behind them or black clouds of rain. It is only the buzzing of the police helicopter which finally shifts her. She cannot stand its drone and can't get used to it, though it is a constant presence, scouring the streets of Govan for clusters of men with baseball bats, for youths with meandering gaits.

Lorraine reaches the first tenement block on the corner of West Prince's Street and peers at the buzzers by the security door. She looks for one marked Kerry Clugston.

Kerry works in the box office with Lorraine. She is a wiry woman. Her hair is cropped short and it clings to her small face. Her jaw clicks when she speaks and she has appeared as a Thunderbird puppet in Lorraine's dreams. She's a nippy sweetie, a particularly nasty one, and likes to poke fun at everything earthbound, excluding herself.

Her passion is for star formations and planets and meteorites and spacemen and rockets and black holes. She buys limited edition models of the Starship Enterprise. She watches tapes of *Blake's Seven* over and over. She spends hundreds purchasing photographic originals of UFO sightings and astronaut ephemera. She thinks it normal and reasonable, and turns an angry scarlet if mocked.

This is the third Fantasy Space Party Kerry has held and the first Lorraine has attended. Lorraine presses her buzzer and jumps when Kerry screeches from her top-flat window – 'Look at you!'

Lorraine blinks. Kerry leans through her open window. Her face is plastered with platinum. A large silver antenna protrudes from her forehead. It waggles excitedly.

Lorraine points to the security door. 'Let me in, Kerry,' she pleads. Her voice is soft and wimpish, and she is unable to tell whether Kerry doesn't hear or pretends not to. Especially when Kerry replies.

'Would you like me to let you in?'

Someone taps Lorraine on her shoulder. She starts and turns to face her boss, volatile Gloria the box-office manager, great one minute, shouting crazy the next. Lorraine likes her. Without Gloria the box office would be gloomier still.

'For fuck's sake, Kerry, what a stupid question!' shouts Gloria.

The Victoria's box office is windowless and as dark and dreary as a cellar. It was once a store room for costumes and props, until wardrobe and set design were moved to a grander building three streets away.

It is painted the same muddy brown as the theatre's exterior, and its walls curve. Customers smile when they enter it. They think it is cosy like a hamster's nest. It's hard to get them to leave, especially if they are old and it's snowing out.

Lorraine finds it claustrophobic. She can only tell the time of day by looking at her watch. She can only tell the weather by looking at the customers' clothing. It's worse if she's on winter late shift or early shift, because then she moves from the dark outside to the dark of the office and it seems as if there is no such thing as light and sun and air. It makes her lethargic and her skin yellow.

Gloria tries her best to enliven it. She buys bunches of flowers with the petty cash and arranges them in art deco vases on the table near the flier rack. She changes the event posters, making sure none are tatty or out of date. And she dresses in shiny white.

Lorraine watches her flit busily about, day in day out, like a large white moth trapped in a box. A sturdy, determined moth which refuses to notice its wings are fraying, its beautiful glossy body powder is dropping to the floor.

Gloria wears white tonight, her voluptuous form crammed inside a snow-white catsuit. A chunky metal zip travels from her crotch over the three hills of her stomach, the mountain range which is her chest, up to the fleshy goitre of her neck. A slinky purple ski hat sits on her head. 'I know what you're thinking,' she says to Lorraine. 'But who's the expert here?

Kerry? Has she ever met an extraterrestrial?'

'Probably,' says Lorraine. 'She probably picnics with them at weekends.'

Gloria bounds up the close stairs and strides into Kerry's flat. Lorraine follows slowly. She clings to the banister, pulls herself up step by step.

Kerry has decorated the close. She's taped Athena posters of the heavens and photographs of sputniks, comsats and skylabs over the bottle-green and scarlet Victorian wall tiles. Hippy tin mobiles of moons and stars dangle from the frames of the stairwell windows. Lorraine thinks of primary schools as she edges by.

'Oh my,' calls Kerry from her open door. 'The Earth's atmosphere doesn't suit you.'

'It's my Cellophane,' replies Lorraine, reaching the landing. 'I've wrapped it too tight. I can't move very fast.'

'Sshh,' smiles Kerry. She circles a pinkie in the air, then tweaks the lobes of Lorraine's ears. 'Your alien energy is being depleted. Don't waste it.'

Lorraine was scheduled to work a twelve-hour stint at the box office today. She was to clerk until 9.00 p.m., which gave her an excuse to avoid Kerry's cosmic celebration. But then the evening's solo performance of virtuoso trumpeting was cancelled – the performer had fallen off his tour bus, smashed his front teeth – and Lorraine wasn't required to cover interval sales. Kerry reissued her invite and Lorraine was obliged to accept.

Lorraine is useless at eventing and socializing. She can't understand why she finds it so difficult, why she only goes out when forced.

When she first moved to Glasgow, when she was feeling happy and her enthusiasm was high, even then she couldn't arrange anything for herself, she couldn't get it together.

She didn't even see the one show she really wanted to.

Lorraine had no idea who the dance group was, had never heard of the choreographer. The poster advertising the show attracted her, six female dancers in pinafores and T-shirts. They were holding their pinafores high and were strutting their stuff, their limbs disciplined and perfect. They looked like they were enjoying themselves, dancing so well together, keeping in time, displaying their taut bodies, their motivation and purpose.

She's only been out when bullied, when she's been dragged straight from work to long drinking sessions with her colleagues, to first-night parties with cliquey camp actors. Dreadful evenings which have made her feel more lonely, more isolated, less inclined to adventure beyond the damp walls and barred windows of her cellar flat. Dreadful evenings which are repeated regularly, which Lorraine never escapes because she is unable to assert herself, because somewhere inside her she hopes perhaps this time it'll be different, perhaps this time it'll be the start of something important, wild, good.

Lorraine ladles Kerry's 'Paraselene Punch' into a polystyrene cup. The punch smells of antiseptic. It is urine-coloured and has apple slices cut into moon and star shapes floating on its slimy surface. Lorraine holds her nose and tips it back.

'It'll ruin your beautiful blue skin,' says Ruari Lane, Gloria's deputy. He is wearing a gorilla outfit and a placard around his neck which reads 'Planet Of The Apes. Natch!' He holds a can of beer in his furry mits.

'My funeral,' mumbles Lorraine.

Ruari interviewed Lorraine. Gloria offered her a job, and Ruari interviewed her just in case, just in case she was bad or mad or ugly.

He greeted her at the stage door, then took her up a winding staircase to the Hospitality Room. Lorraine was impressed. The Hospitality Room is plush. With a crystal chandelier and a ceiling rose as big as a dining table. The best room in the theatre, used to entertain sponsors: short men in grey suits with their tall, young wives; short men who own printing companies, insurance companies, pet-food factories, who donate thousands to keep the theatre from sinking into a redder red.

Ruari offered Lorraine a seat, then sat close beside her. He made her feel shy. He was dressed in a sharp black suit, grey shirt and spotted navy and white tie. His hair was brushed back from his crown. He looked leonine, hungry and tasty. Lorraine blushed as he grasped her hands. 'Very nice,' he said to her. 'I'm glad your hair is up. We like a professional image. Yes, clean, smart and pretty, very very pretty.'

He asked Lorraine to have a drink with him, but she declined. She felt it wasn't right. She felt she shouldn't become intimate with her boss and she didn't want to date. He asked her again some weeks later and again she declined – with more force this time – because she'd learnt a lot about Ruari. He is a chancer, a shallow-case, someone whose soul has taken a walk.

Kerry's tingling ambience music ends. It drifts out with a chorus of whispers – 'Ooohhh. Aaahhh. Ooohh.' Kerry wafts across the room to select the next CD. *The War of the Worlds*. She feeds it into her player, turning it up high. Then she bellows over the intro, 'Come on space cadets! Let's boogie!'

Lorraine grimaces, and catches sight of Nicky, another work colleague, slumped against the far wall. He is dressed as Captain Kirk. His lean body looking tidy and fit in a tight blue jersey and black trousers. He smiles at her and mouths 'Help!' Then Kerry grabs him by the arm and pulls him to dance.

Kerry moves around him in her outfit of ethereal gauze, her silver antenna wiggling ecstatically. 'Come on. Your centre of gravity has been displaced, you are floating, your head feels light. Come on. Come on,' she urges.

Slowly the entire party rises to dance. Lorraine is not sure whether from embarrassment, fear or drunkenness. Ruari jigs around her and Lorraine, despite herself, also finds she's moving, shuffling awkwardly because her costume won't allow for anything more.

'Shake it baby,' smarms Ruari. He dips his head towards Lorraine, then throws it back. He repeats the movement four or five times, then stops to unzip his gorilla suit. He licks his lips. His sparse clutch of chest hairs springs free, and his small naked paunch.

The same paunch which protrudes beneath his work shirt and over the waistband of his neatly pressed trousers as he struts around the box office. Lorraine stares at it. It is surprisingly firm, like a tightly rolled towel, and nestled in its centre is his belly button – a small domestic hollow which has caught the fluff and detritus of the day. It reminds Lorraine of Jenny. Jenny who lives with Ruari. Jenny who visits the box office now and then wanting Ruari to go shopping for a settee or a carpet, for wallpaper or for those glass lampshades which are shaped like bluebells.

Lorraine enters Kerry's yellow bathroom. She fills the tiny handbasin and stares at her reflection in the oval mirror before her. The blue dye on her face is streaked, almost non-existent on her sweatiest parts – her forehead, the ridge of her nose, her chin. Some of the dye has spread into her hair. Her washing-up gloves flap limply from her headband.

The bathroom walls are plasterboard and Lorraine can hear everything beyond. She can hear people shuffling in and out of the kitchen to get more drink. She can hear giggles and whispers and sighs as Kerry runs a slide show in her living room. It is education-time.

Kerry's parties are famous for their slide shows. Kerry is an enthusiast who has to share her enthusiasm. She has to instruct. She has to impart. And so she's halted the revelry to show slides of Neptune and Venus and Mars. She's hushed the jollifications for a question and answer plenary.

95

Lorraine wonders if she can escape, if she can sneak from the party without Kerry noticing. As she leaves her reflection she wipes her wet hands down the front of her Cellophane. They squeak, leave finger smears on her breasts.

'Oh, sorry,' says Nicky. He stands framed in the doorway, his arms raised in the air as if in surrender.

Lorraine tries to squeeze by him. 'It's OK. Don't worry.'

'But I am worried,' says Nicky. He moves quickly to trap her. His body is hot and she doesn't resist it. 'I think you've been avoiding me.'

Lorraine and Nicky have kissed. Once. Two months ago. When they were left alone together to close the box office. Slowly they counted the cash, checked the print-outs, locked the safe. Slowly they skirted each other, until the lights went out.

A power cut.

Lorraine screamed, and Nicky put his arms around her. He whispered, 'Ring my bell! You're trembling.' Then he kissed her.

Nicky is a tall man. He is dark like an Italian. He has black hair, black eyelashes, thick stubble grows over his chin, and his hirsute shoulders and chest are visible beneath his expensive tailored shirts. He is Italianate, but has bad teeth and his eyes are covered with grey film and he has a catch phrase – 'Ring my bell' – which he says often, too often.

The kiss surprised Lorraine. It was agreeable and persuasive. She could feel herself getting wet, and probably would have gone further if the lights hadn't suddenly flickered on and revealed them to be Lorraine and Nicky, workmates, box-office clerks.

Nicky removed his hands from her breasts and hurried home. Lorraine locked the box office, waved goodbye to security at stage door and sat on the Govan bus shaking.

Lorraine has been down the romance route before. She has kissed and cuddled and fucked and shared. She has been

96

engaged to the boy-next-door. It has never eased her restlessness, her dissatisfaction.

The next day she ignored Nicky, and the next. He tried to get her to talk to him, to go to the pub with him, to mull it over. But Lorraine refused. She didn't want to court it. Love. Disappointing love. She didn't want to add to her discontent.

But now she's not so sure, because Nicky likes her, and her body likes him, whatever her head says. And today she realized she might really want him.

The work's clock ticked towards 3.00 p.m. as Gloria came from the screen which shields the back of the office from the customers. 'Kerry,' she shouted. 'Leave your filing. We need to discuss a discrepancy.'

'Surprise! Surprise!' whispered Nicky to Lorraine. He sat with her on the front counter, waiting for customers to serve. It was a slow afternoon.

Lorraine shifted on her high stool and quietly laughed.

'What's so funny?' asked Nicky.

'Life,' said Lorraine. She tapped her fingers on the computer keyboard. 'Life is funny.'

'Tell me about it,' said Nicky. He yawned a wide yawn and, folding his arms, slumped over the counter.

'Sweet dreams,' said Lorraine.

She stared beyond her computer at the curved wall of the box office. She barely noticed the mess of posters and leaflets stuck there, scattered along the seating and display rack. Her eyes skimmed the office, lingered on its hefty wooden door, as she considered what it would be like to have money, to be able to dress like the women who sit in the first circle on opera nights, to have the freedom and choice which money brings.

The box-office door opened and Lorraine gradually registered a customer. She was very thin, with muscular arms, man-sized hands. She entered the office with a sexual swagger. Lorraine began to feel nervous. She knew her from the poster of the six dancers; the show which she'd wanted to see but hadn't.

The woman leant against the counter. She wore a summery slip. It had slender shoulder straps and a low front. Her chest was hard, her shoulders bulky like a swimmer's. Lorraine eyed the tight flesh.

'I need some assistance,' the woman said, her voice husky and resonant.

Lorraine nodded. She opened her mouth to reply, but was distracted by Nicky. He'd raised his head, was pushing a thick hand through his thick hair. A flirtatious smile flushed his lips.

Lorraine recognized the smile. He'd used it on her. She thought it was exclusively hers.

'What kind of assistance?' He smiled.

Kerry shows off the luminous map of the heavens which she's painted on her living-room ceiling. The room is dark. The lights are out and Kerry trails a sparkly pointer over representations of Charles's Wain, the Big Dipper, Cassiopeia's Chair, Orion.

A man is using the blackout as a chance to molest. He crawls around the room falling against women, touching any protruding body parts. He grabs Lorraine's ankle and she struggles to object.

'Fuck off,' she mumbles, as Gloria blasts the air with drunken singing.

'Please release me. Let me go,' she wails.

Then, 'Christ,' whispers Nicky, sitting close to Lorraine. 'Let's find the bedroom.'

Nicky and Lorraine hold on to each other as they scan Kerry's collection of model spaceships. The silvery coloured plastic ships dangle from threads attached to the bedroom ceiling. On her dressing table is a rocket made from a washing-up bottle, the cups of an egg carton forming its boosters.

'Do you think she's retarded?' whispers Nicky.

'Well, she likes you,' Lorraine replies, waddling for the bed. It's covered with coats and bags. Lorraine struggles to throw them on the floor. Nicky comes across to help her.

'Ring my bell!' he exclaims as Kerry's bedspread is revealed.

The bedspread depicts Neil Armstrong. His wholesome clear face looks into the distance as images of the moon float around him. Nicky climbs on to the bed and lies across the astronaut.

Lorraine joins Nicky. She places her head on his shoulder. He begins to play with her rubber gloves. 'Tell me about you, Lorraine,' he whispers.

'Me? I don't trust me,' Lorraine blurts. She looks into Nicky's eyes. They are bleary. The grey film which covers them has thickened. She can see his pupils moving beneath the film. They resemble tadpoles skidding in a murky pond. She can't tell if he sees things properly. She can't tell if he sees her. She feels uneasy as she confides further.

'I'm not very happy,' she says.

Lorraine moved to Glasgow in late 1989. She spent New Year's Eve alone. She sat in her flat drinking Bailey's and eating chocolate Swiss roll, watching Scottish television embarrass itself with men in kilts, Gaelic folk songs, long shots of Glasgow's George Square and predictions for the forthcoming Year of Culture, and Scottish artistes famous in Scotland but unheard of elsewhere.

There was a lot of noise coming from her street. The police helicopter was hovering overhead. Somebody was having a party, playing Republican songs and shouting, 'Kill the bastards.' Children were squealing and women were singing country and western tunes, 'd.i.v.o.r.c.e.' and 'Crystal Chandelier'. Then 'Oohh. Aahh', everything seemed to hush and the sound of popping fireworks pulled Lorraine downstairs.

She stood on the street corner with her cardigan wrapped tightly around her, watching the fireworks welcome in 1990.

They were on the other side of the Clyde, somewhere in the West End, but it was still spectacular, it still seemed like the Year of Culture really was for everybody.

It was a beautiful night, dark and cool. The fireworks went on and on, blue and purple spirals, white fountains, red pokers, spinning wheels, rockets, stars. A lilac explosion, then a pink, then a bright bright gold and green.

'Lovely, hen,' said a large man with a child on his shoulders. And it was lovely, the loveliest thing. Lorraine returned indoors not wanting to go to bed, because she felt so opened and hopeful.

It didn't take long to feel weighed down. She had to sell tickets for shows few people wanted to see. She had to learn to pronounce the names of foreign theatre companies to avoid being corrected by the culture snobs in the know. She had to explain over and over to customers why the best seats in the house are always given to sponsors for the most popular shows – the musicals, the comedies – why the theatre continues to sell tickets for seats which are placed behind poles or at the side of poles. 'Restricted view,' said one customer. 'There was no view. All I saw was a pole and I've seen better poles, I've opened my legs to better poles.'

Nicky picks at the sticky tape which holds together Lorraine's fancy dress. 'What you need,' he says, 'is a good man.'

'Perhaps,' Lorraine replies, and she watches as Nicky begins to unwind her. He slides his hands under the first layer of Cellophane, before rolling her over, then over again.

Lorraine feels her body start to breathe, her skin expand. A strong sweaty smell escapes to meet Nicky's aftershave, and she tucks her hands under her armpits to hide it, but Nicky pulls them free, nuzzles into her and sniffs.

'Ring my bell!' he says. 'Animal!'

He takes her underarm hair in his mouth, sucks at its wetness. He reaches for the straps of her swimsuit. He eases the straps off her shoulders, down past her elbows. The suit drops to sit on her waist.

'Mmmm.' Nicky cups her naked breasts, moves his thumbs across her nipples till Lorraine feels them tingle and raise. She reaches for the zip of his trousers.

Lorraine lost her virginity to her next-door neighbour, a red-haired boy who was crazy about motorbike racing.

He had a stack of racing souvenirs in his bedroom. Trophies and medals and photographs and a helmet. The helmet was battered and buckled. A faint pink discoloured the webbing inside, and as the boy removed her clothes, slipped her breasts free from her teen bra, Lorraine wondered if the man who'd worn it had survived.

Kerry is playing *Ziggy Stardust*. David Bowie's voice cries high and plaintive. It seeps from the living room into the bedroom. Nicky moves his hands inside the crotch of Lorraine's costume. He begins to rub her.

Lorraine feels tingling sensations and briefly she goes with them. She rises, sinks down, rises. She knows if Nicky persists she will come.

She lifts herself free. Nicky lies on his back looking up at her. His mouth is slack. His lips parted to reveal uneven, smoke-grained teeth. 'What's the problem?' he asks.

'No problem,' Lorraine replies.

She reaches for Nicky's balls, weighs them in her hands. Then she takes his penis, pulls the gusset of her swimsuit to one side and inserts him. She moves to David Bowie, picking up an unavoidable rhythm.

'Ring my bell!' Nicky whispers. 'This is the best.' He reaches up to pull off Lorraine's headband. He throws it to the floor and Lorraine hears the soft slap of the rubber gloves as they hit a vinyl bag. She loses her concentration, glances up to catch her reflection in Kerry's dressing-table mirror.

She is startled, surprised by what she sees. In her swimsuit she is lithe, athletic. Its Lycra clings tight to her behind, clasps her thin waist. Her naked breasts sit high; her nipples ruddy and erect. Her long hair trails down her back, wisps over her shoulders. The blue paint covering her limbs and face has faded to a complimentary sheen. She shines aquatic, a diver caught in a watery shimmer. She moves up and down on Nicky, watching her body work him.

'Ohh!' moans Nicky. The shaft of his penis is visible in the mirror. Lorraine raises herself until it nearly slips from her, but not quite. Gently, slowly she circles above him, tickling the tip with the edge of her hole.

'Ring my bell!' Nicky groans. 'Ring my bell!'

Lorraine throws her head forward, then back. She watches her hair shower in the air, and through its soft and silky sound she hears David Bowie sing his final note; Kerry, Ruari, Gloria and the others screeching in the room next door.

Lorraine drops to take Nicky's cock inside her. And she is making him so mad for her, she is so good, that she wishes she had more than the mirror. She wishes she had an audience. Because this performance deserves an audience. She deserves an audience.

Lorraine has a recurring dream. She stands alone on a stage – a large raised stage with an elaborate, beautifully painted proscenium arch – and she recites an epic poem. The poem is difficult. It's written in archaic language. There are long complicated words and phrases. The meaning is hard to find and to convey. But Lorraine is doing well, very well. She's wearing a simple black dress, her face is white, her eyes outlined with black pencil. Her whole demeanour says 'Concentrate on the poem. The poem is important.' Her voice is mellifluous, magical. It encourages laughter, anger, tears. The large auditorium stretched before her is packed with men, women and children. They clap and shout and scream and give her a standing ovation at the finish.

Lorraine collects the flowers they've thrown at her feet, gathers them in her arms, plunges her head into the blooms to sniff their ripe pungent smell. She dances off the stage feeling transcendent, whole and complete, steady in herself, happy.

Until she bumps into a crowd of Thunderbird puppets congregating in the wings. Too many of them, all with Kerry Clugston's face and clacking jaw. They snap through her blissfulness, wake her sharpish, and she opens her eyes to register her surroundings, her real and worthless world.

Lorraine and Nicky lie next to each other. Above them float the spaceships, their plastic bodies flimsy and light. They sway in the soft evening breeze which blows through the open bedroom window and as they sway they fill the room with a fluttering, a brisk-winged noise which reminds Lorraine of the box office, of Gloria's neurotic busyness.

Next door Elton John sings 'Rocket Man'. Kerry and a few party-goers accompany him. Their voices are harsh and unlovely. Lorraine turns to Nicky . 'I feel cold,' she says.

He smiles at her. She can see spittle on his lips, the yellowness of his teeth. His chin is firm and dotted with black stubble. She shivers as he takes her in his arms.

'I'll warm you,' he says. He rubs his hairy chest against her breasts. 'Ring my bell. This is nice. Don't you think so?'

He runs his hands along Lorraine's shoulders. Her flesh chills to his touch and she pushes against him to break the embrace. She pulls up the straps of her swimsuit.

'I'm going,' she says. She climbs off the bed and feels on the floor for her flip flops, fumbles to put them on.

Nicky reaches out to stop her. Lorraine grabs a coat from the pile on the floor and thrusts her arms in the sleeves. 'But that's not yours!' Nicky shouts as Lorraine leaves the room.

Lorraine closes the security door, steps into the brightly lit street. It is very late. A hush hangs in the air. It deepens as Lorraine walks from Kerry's tenement, escaping the sounds of men and women drunk and pretending to be other beings, aliens from more exotic planets.

She turns down an alley and breaks into a run. She hears the slap slap of her flip flops as they smack on the cobbles. She feels dewy damp tickling her toes, Nicky's wetness on her legs. She pulls the stranger's coat warmer around her.

At the end of the alleyway there is a zebra crossing. The yellow globes which mark the crossing sit in the night sky like moons. Lorraine eyes their glossy rounds. They remind her of the lollipops she used to suck as a child. She recalls the hard knob of sweet as it clacked against her teeth, the taste of gooey sugar and fruit.

She stands on the kerb, her flip flops curling over its edge. She rocks gently, secure in the coat as a sprightly Glasgow wind begins to pester the street. There are no cars and she is miles from home. The crossing flashes a green man and starts to beep. But Lorraine remains standing, crosses slowly, deliberately, on red.

Cat Talk

The cat is enviably agile. Its bones are loose knit, allowing it to weave and crouch and squeeze through the smallest chink.

The time I leave from work varies, which is why I can't always catch the 5.30. Some days this is a blessing. The 5.30 bus is packed, always full of smoke, always hell to get off.

The stop nearest my house is the first after a roundabout. When the bus is empty there's hardly a problem. But when the bus is full, like the 5.30, it's murder. The standing passengers hold tight as the bus goes into a swerve. They won't budge to let me down the aisle.

The 5.30 has this attraction though: three women who talk about cats. They are all over fifty, dress in similar brown macs with tie belts. Two of them have the standard perm, whilst the one who does most of the talking models a tube-like bun. It sits on the top of her head, a beckoning receiver drawing and emitting news about cats.

I first heard them on Day 1 of the Gulf War. The bus was unusually silent, except for a few voices worrying whether Saddam would send terrorists into Scotland, except for the women talking about cats. I was surprised nobody told the women to shut up. It seemed like they were committing a crime, bemoaning hair balls as young men prepared for death.

But I've begun to appreciate them. You can submerge yourself in cat flu, kitten fever, the merits of name tags and elasticated collars. You can forget the real crappiness of life.

Provide your cat with a clean sanitary tray which is large enough for it to stand inside and deep enough to hold plenty of litter for burying. Wash the tray once a week.

I work in a department store behind a perfume counter. But I was made for better things. At school I was the brightest in the class, and the most popular. I had prospects. Then I met Danny. He was down from Scotland on holiday. I met him at a disco and my hormones went wild. I gave up everything to move to Glasgow, to be with a twenty-seven-year-old turning to fat, a market trader into cracked crockery and melamine.

The marriage was OK for a while. But then I got bored. It's all routine: the missionary position, the sock-washing on Sunday, the fish supper on Friday. Danny has no idea. He thinks we're fine. He thinks I love him.

But for the past five years I've had affairs. I see the men at my work, as they sniff the perfumes and fantasize, and I muscle my way in, offer more than a squirt of Obsession. I go for the weedy type, with hopeless hair. Because they let me get on top. Because they talk to me about life. Because they give me pleasure.

My current lover is Bob. He's been around for a while, because he makes me laugh. At least he used to. But now the world is getting so unstable he's changed.

On Day 1 of the Gulf War he came into the shop to give me a box of chocolates. 'For you,' he said, 'because I love you in that white tunic, because I cherish everything about you.'

'Oh Bob,' I smiled. 'You should be a stand-up.'

'A stand-up?' he asked.

'Comedian,' I explained.

'I'm serious,' he said.

If your cat's behaviour suddenly alters examine the cat carefully: it may be ill.

Bob hung his angular face over the 99p toilet waters. He was furious. 'Bob,' I said. 'The chocolates are lovely, you are lovely, but I'm married.'

'But what if it comes to conscription?' he snarled. 'What if I have to go away? I will want to know you're mine.'

'This is desperation talking, Bob,' I said. I felt as if I'd entered a movie. 'There will be no conscription.'

Now we're into Week 3 and Bob is almost manic. He's obsessed with conscription, but more – a black hole has entered him. He can no longer study. He has stopped washing. He eats only bread, drinks only water.

Part of me enjoys his despair: the sex is amazing. But mainly I can't do with it. He pesters me at work. He walks me to the bus stop, clutching tightly at my hands. I get no relief unless I can catch the 5.30 and listen to the women who talk about cats.

Do not keep frail and senile cats alive merely because you cannot face a trip to the vet's.

Bob comes into work. He arrives at 12 o'clock, which is his regular time. He looks terrible. He wears his green winter pullover; it has holes beneath the arms and a large oily streak runs from the neck edge across his chest. His trousers are black, but even they look dirty. They hang limp from his skinny frame. And he has shaved his head. He hasn't touched his beard, but has removed his mop of cotted hair. I feel sympathy for him, but also anger. Everybody else manages to go about their own business, to get on with life, why can't he? Why does he have to be so melodramatic?

'Bob,' I say. 'I've had enough. I'm not cut out for this.'

'What?' he whispers. 'Are you dumping me?'

'I'm sorry, Bob. But it's not like it was. I used to look up to you. And we had fun. But now I feel so responsible. And I can't stand the gloom. I have problems of my own. I can't cope with yours too.'

This morning I tucked into my Rice Krispies, fuelling my-self for another stretch in the shop. Rex strolled in to start his begging act. He's Danny's Alsatian and I loathe him. He has bad breath. He sat in front of me and thumped his large tail on the carpet. Little flecks of gravel jumped from the pile and I was reminded of Danny's work boots; the sturdy steel-capped boots he wears in case rain or hurricane hits his stall. I shiv-ered. I've seen lots of those boots, on the news. They belong to soldiers, the successful ones, who walk and run and tramp their boots over the bodies of others.

Danny cheers the news: he cheers the soldiers; and the images of oil wells alight; the bombed out families; the Scuds; the POWs. He's a thug, which is why I'm still bound to him.

'So you're dumping me,' says Bob. He stands a while with his head cocked like some stupid bird, then he walks out of the shop.

'Thank God,' says Marjorie, the Max Factor woman. 'He gave me the creeps.'

Do not make a stud out of a tom with ingrowing eyelashes, inverted eyelids and/or a kinked tail. Also check that the tom has a pair of nicely hung testicles. Neuter if in doubt.

I catch the 5.30 bus and the only seat spare is next to the women who talk about cats. I listen to their chat. It helps me forget Bob's naked head, his look of hurt.

'All I know is my Uncle George passes away, and the next minute this little ginger stray lands on my doorstep. I pick him up and what do I see? Uncle George's eyes. The same old gentleman eyes. "Well," I say to this kitten, "do you mind if I call you George?"' The woman with the tube-like bun taps her cigarette; the ash falls on her coat and she brushes it away. Her expression is serious. I want to hug her for it.

When I get home, Danny is waiting for me. I know something

is wrong, because he has switched off the news. 'I've had a phone call,' he says, 'from somebody called Bob. Claims he knows you and is madly in love with you.'

I try to keep calm, to act innocent. 'Bob?' I say. I shake my head. 'I don't know any Bob.'

Cats can be nervous. They are frightened by loud noises and bangs.

I go to bed early, leaving Danny to watch some newscaster move plastic model battleships over a map of the Gulf. He is raging, but he hasn't hit me. His hand has just hovered close to my face. 'You wouldn't live,' he said, 'if I started on you now.'

I slip off my work overall and pull on my nightie. I curl into bed and try to decide what to do. Nothing comes into my head except for Bob. 'You selfish fucker,' I say aloud. 'You selfish, selfish fucker.'

I sleep fitfully, my dreams frantic. I'm running down corridors, sliding down helter skelters. I'm a little brown sparrow being chased by a big brown eagle. I'm on fire. I toss and turn, and only truly settle when I realize Danny won't be joining me.

There is a loud knock on the bedroom door in the morning. It wakes me, and I rise not in a sleepy way but tensed. 'Yes,' I say.

Danny saunters in. He seems pleased with himself. He holds a tray, piled with two plates and two cups of tea. On the plates are slabs of plain bread and square sausage. I feel queasy, especially when he fixes this smile on me. 'I thought we could have breakfast together, have a chat before you go to work. Sort out a few things.'

The cat doesn't have nine lives, it just has very loose skin. Many a cat has recovered quickly from an accident or fight, because the skin has behaved like a great big coat slipping and sliding to protect the organs beneath.

*

'What's happened to you?' says Marjorie the Max Factor woman.

'Ran into a lamppost,' I reply, pulling down my overall sleeve to try to hide the bruises. They stand out red and impressive against my fair skin, and no amount of foundation will disguise them.

'Some lamppost,' says Marjorie, whistling.

I wait for her to pry further, but a customer interrupts. The rest of the day is lost, to sales, to stock-taking, to dusting the bottles of perfume which have stood behind the counter for years. At 12 o'clock I watch for Bob, expecting him to come with apologies, begging for forgiveness and to start again. But there is no Bob.

I am not upset. I would've liked the chance to lay into him, but know he's not worth it. I imagine him cowering in the corner of his bedsit, listening to the World Service, crossing his fingers that conscription is not an item. Poor Bob. I'm not as puny as him.

Cats are survivors.

I step on to the 5.30 and follow the queue of people up the metal stairs to the top deck. The bus is packed, but I get the seat I want, next to the three women who talk about cats. They are mid-way through a conversation on defleaing, and I interrupt.

The words tumble out. 'Hiya,' I say. 'Can I butt in? It's just that I have a cat and she's covered in ticks. I've tried all the powders, but they only make her ill. And I've washed her and washed her, and of course she doesn't like that.'

The three women look at me. They are on the defensive, suspecting ridicule. I try to appear harmless. I smile, will their acceptance.

'No, cats don't like water,' says one of the women. She glances at her friends.

The woman with the tube-like bun backs her. 'But they are

fascinated by it,' she comments. 'My Molly likes nothing better than to sit and watch me in the bath. She likes me to raise my knees, so she can see the water trickle off them. Sometimes she even licks the water off.'

'Well, what do you suggest I do?' I implore. 'I'm getting quite desperate. Should I have my whole house fumigated? Should I have Tinkerbell put down?'

'No. Never,' says the woman with the tube-like bun. She seems outraged. 'There's too much death and destruction in this world as it is. Just ask the vet for a spray, not a powder. Sprays stay put.'

I feel the curving motion of the bus and look out of the window to see my stop go by. I blanch, but do not move. Instead I peer at the familiar scenery of shops and Chinese take-away, and hold my breath.

'Excuse me,' says one of the women who talks about cats. 'I don't mean to pry, but I'm sure I've seen you on this bus before and you've always got off at the roundabout.'

'No,' I say. 'No, I live in Greenock. And I usually travel by car, but it's broken down and my husband's not around to mend it. He's in the Gulf, poor thing.'

Hundreds of cats disappear. Most of them go at night, and their owners never see them again.

Danny was like a leech this morning, sticking to me as I prepared for work. I couldn't take a suitcase. I couldn't take my building society book, or the necklace my grandma left me. He checked my pockets, cleaned out my handbag before returning it to my shoulder. 'It's not that I don't trust you, Christine,' he said, handing me a lipstick, fifty pence and my travel card.

As the bus journeys to Greenock, I watch the unfamiliar territory and refuse to feel frightened. The woman with the tube-like bun sits beside me. She waves goodbye to her companions as they get off at Woodhall. 'Ciao miaow,' she calls.

111

'Ciao miaow,' they reply.

'Now,' she says, turning to look at me. Her face is covered with a fine pink powder; it smells of baby talc. 'What shall we do with you?'

Cats are perceptive. They have a sixth sense which enables them to read situations for what they really are.

The time I leave from work varies, but I always make sure I catch the 5.30. The 5.30 is always packed, always full of smoke. But it has this attraction. My three friends who talk about cats. Thelma, Jean and Doris.

Doris sports the tube-like bun. I suggested she get rid of the bun. On my first night in her home I mentioned a good hairdresser's. She told me to lay off. She is blunt, but kind. She pulled the plug on the news when she saw it was bothering me, and she gave me comfrey ointment for my bruises. She also let me talk about Danny and Bob. But not now.

'There comes a point,' she says, 'when you have to change the record. Men don't make a conversation. Cats do.'

Hair so Black

I check myself in the bathroom mirror. My fine, grey hair is scraped in a bun. My face free of make-up. I look naked, old, as if I've been pickled. My only concession to ornamentation is a pair of earrings: silver drops like solidified tears.

This is a bad day for me. The day my friend and neighbour, Daphne Carter, is to be buried.

I was with Daphne when she died. We were sitting side by side on her sofa watching a wildlife programme. She reached across my lap for her knitting. She was knitting some awful multicoloured coat. And she collapsed. Her head falling heavy on my stomach.

'Daphne!' I cried. 'What are you playing at!'

When she said nothing, I began to stroke her hair. I ran my fingers through the glorious curls. I cooed gently. My actions surprised me. I lost control later that afternoon.

During my last year at primary a boy locked me in a shed. The shed was at the rear of his father's allotment. It was damp, cobbled together from old floorboards and doors. It had no window. As soon as the boy pushed me inside and slid the bolt, I began to panic. I didn't scream. I was unable to scream. I just gulped large gulps of air, one after the other, fast. It was like I was trying to gather in as much breath as possible to pre-serve myself. It sent me dizzy. I blacked out and fell to the grassy floor.

I did the same four hours after Daphne's death. My doctor, a large useless man, tried to comfort me. He told me it was natural, said it was nothing to worry about. 'Like an exorcism,' he explained. 'You'll feel much better for it.'

He was wrong. The days between Daphne's death and her burial have been terrible. Her departure has carved a hole inside me. Like my innards have been scooped. She was only fifty-six. Her going has made me more aware of my own mortality. But worse. It has left me exposed. Suddenly I have nothing. No friend. No one to turn to. No one to chat with about the past. I flounder, only able to decide on one thing. I cannot attend the funeral.

I place my basket of provisions on Daphne's back doorstep. I feel in my cardigan pocket for the key, insert it in the lock, turn it slowly. I shiver, not knowing what to expect.

The door swings open, revealing Daphne's kitchen. It is a small kitchen. The floor is covered with red and white lino. The fridge is white, the cooker brown. The units are second hand, not fitted. Daphne hated her kitchen, thought it shabby. But she'd never done anything about it, preferring to concentrate her energies on her knitting and her vegetable patch.

I pick up my basket, enter the kitchen. I know I am being foolish, but the sameness of everything makes me wait for Daphne. I look towards the hall. I anticipate her welcoming smile and her golden voice.

'Come in, Audrey.'

The way she made my name sound special.

'Come in, Audrey. Tell us all about it.'

I shudder when I realize she's not coming from the living room with a ball of wool in one hand, a cup of tea in the other, or clomping down the stairs to greet me. I shudder when I realize the house is empty. Unfleshed air surrounds me.

I turn my back to the hall, busy myself. I unload my basket. I place a carton of crackers, slab of cheese, tin of cocktail sausages, tin of pineapple, box of cocktail sticks, home-made prawn and egg quiche and a plate of peanut cookies on a worktop.

I run a hand along the worktop. It's been scrubbed, not very well. A powdery scum of cleanser coats the Formica, obscuring its pattern. Jeff's doing.

Jeff is Daphne's son. He is thirty-five years old. He has olive skin and hair so black it looks dyed. He resembles Elvis, the plump version.

Jeff is spoilt. Daphne mothered him, till he was unable to think for himself. Then she began to resent his clinging. She tried to pass him on to me. But I said 'No', which led to an argument.

I had to tell Jeff about his mother's death, and I expected tears, panic. I expected him to ask, 'Well, what is going to happen to me? Who's going to look after me?' But his fleshy face never altered. And unlike me he feels able to attend the funeral. He seems quite cold. I guess he's not losing sleep; I guess he's not dreaming my dream.

The past few nights I have dreamt of being an astronaut, abandoned by ship and colleagues. There I am floating aimlessly among the unreal stars, arms and legs akimbo, eyes petrified.

Jeff promised to leave me a note. I glance round the kitchen and find one attached to the fridge door, held in place by a magnetic figure. The figure is of a jolly snowman, with orange nose and little black eyes. I pull the note from under him, hating his idiotic smile.

'So good of you to offer to do this,' I read. 'The extra salad stuff, marg and cheese are in the fridge. There's a box of other foodstuffs in the unit by the door. Can understand why you want to give the funeral a miss, but hope you feel able to welcome us back about 2. Looking forward to your lovely tea. Mum always admired your cooking. Jeff.'

I stare at the round childish handwriting, tuck the note in my cardigan pocket. I'm finding it hard. Yes, Daphne always admired my cooking and I shall miss her appreciation, her exclamations of pleasure. She liked sweet things. She liked my trifles and the little sponge cakes I make set in chocolate cases.

I place the last doily on the last plate and load the plate with sausage rolls. I place this plate next to the others. I'm unsure how many will be returning for the tea, but I've made enough for a bus load. Daphne always attracted a crowd.

I have done a good job. My night school in Food Presentation has paid off. Daphne laughed when I registered for the class. She wanted me to do something practical like Car Maintenance. But I wanted something soothing. Food Presentation taught me how to make mouse-shaped jellies, how to turn a simple sandwich into a bread painting. Of course, I haven't used the more frivolous techniques for this tea; just a few touches to make it special. It's my offering to Daphne. A sort of private joke and a farewell gift.

I take the trays and plates of food into Daphne's living room. At the far end of the room lies a big table. The table was a gift from one of Daphne's admirers, her old boss.

Bill, the local pharmacist, employed Daphne from the early days of her widowhood until the day she died. He is a generous man, warm, but too fat. Daphne always used to refer to him as 'too fat'. She used to flirt with him, but had no serious intentions. Bill was useful to her. He fixed her central heating.

I place the food on the table. It looks bare, and so I search in Daphne's tallboy for a cloth. I spy a stack behind a small tin box. The box is embossed with pictures of elephants. It is beautiful, exotic. I haven't seen it before. A dainty key protrudes from a lock in its lid.

I'm not the nosy type. Daphne always used to say, 'Audrey respects others too much.' My restraint is more to do with cowardice, though: I've always been afraid of what may be uncovered. But today I need to keep my mind occupied and besides, this box seems special. I imagine it must hold something important, something which was probably dear to

Daphne and which I could touch, something which may help me to accept my loss. I reach for the key but shiver when I meet its cold metal. Then quickly I push the box aside and pull out a cloth. One of Daphne's Spanish tablecloths.

I flick it open. The cloth is white, decorated with tiny red flowers, green ivy-shaped leaves. Daphne's Spanish tablecloths used to hold bad memories for me. But not now. The passing years have removed their edge.

I went to Spain with Daphne shortly after my husband left. Daphne thought the trip would be therapeutic, believed it would ease my pain. It also gave her an excuse to escape from Jeff. But it was a disaster. I was in no mood for the beach, the country, the charming waiters. Daphne was frustrated, only perked up when she saw the tablecloths. She bought ten. She liked their rustic charm.

I have no idea why my husband left me. We'd been married for twenty years. It had been an unspectacular marriage, no children, no pets, no rows. But it had been pleasant, almost happy. There were days when I was quite thankful for it. At least I wasn't beaten about the head, made to wear kinky costumes, told how to act, speak, think. At least I wasn't classed freakish like Daphne was: a single woman spending her prime alone.

Not that it was Daphne's fault. Fate dealt her a rough hand. Her husband died young, when she was twenty-one, him twenty-three. A crazy man. Always flirting. Always laughing. His death was pathetic. For a time Daphne wanted to dress it up, to make believe he died heroically. But she found his death was common property, not hers to tamper with.

He died at his workplace, Billingston Laundry. He used to put washed and crumpled overalls on to a rack that shunted its way in and out of a steam press. A hot and boring job. But not especially dangerous. 'A freak accident,' the bosses called it, which was fine by Daphne. She never wanted to know how he

117

came to be beneath the mountain of hospital pyjamas, delivered twice weekly from the Southern and General. She joked sometimes that he crawled under there to escape married life. Mickey had been good at Romance, but not the everyday.

The pyjamas suffocated him. He went to his grave marked with impressions of pyjama-top buttons.

Daphne was seven months pregnant when Mickey's coffin was lowered. Her mother-in-law thought it obscene, Daphne standing there with her big belly and rosy glow. She said Daphne could've chopped her hair, looked more distraught.

'Not on your nelly,' replied Daphne, suspecting her motives. Daphne's hair was her best feature. It reached close to her buttocks and was as black as black. Many a man wanted to wrap himself in that hair, including Mickey's father.

Daphne turned to me after the death. She stopped behaving like a polite next-door neighbour and opened up. I welcomed her friendship. I realize now it would never have happened if Mickey had stayed alive. Daphne, despite her independence and strength, was a man's woman, preferred male company. But it was difficult to pursue that interest as a widow. People liked to talk, to cast the first stone. And she had no wish to marry again. 'Marriage is not for me,' she used to say.

The friendship was a good one. Though it got talked about in the early years. Gossips claimed Daphne was using me. For baby-sitting services mostly. But my womb was a mess, had to be removed. There was no way I could have children. So Daphne loaned Jeff to me. It was never spoken about, but I know Daphne had no need to spend every Sunday at the pictures. She did it out of kindness. She did it out of love.

I feel a real warmth when I remember those days. My husband doted on Jeff. We would venture out like a proper family, taking trips to the seaside, visiting the bats at the local zoo. Daphne would sometimes join us. Then it was even more fun. Daphne added excitement, a certain glamour. It was never dull when Daphne came along.

As Jeff grew older, grew more pleasing, things changed. Daphne became overly protective, hid the boy away. I pined, and so did my husband. He would try to catch Jeff on his way to and from school. I would hang over the garden fence desperate to touch the boy's hair, to see his smile. Daphne never revealed why she became so possessive. She said it was one of those things.

The friendship suffered then. It only recovered when my husband went. After the trip to Spain, we would not go a day without seeing each other. We rarely shared intimacies. We just pottered about, watched the television, cooked each other meals, visited the local antiques and crafts fairs. We argued twice.

Daphne said I was too reticent; I countered she was too loud. And then there was her suggestion that I should take Jeff as a lover. As if she couldn't remember the past. As if it didn't count.

But it was a special friendship, like having a close and forgiving relative. I will miss her. My life extends empty. Perhaps I should fill it by joining one of those over-fifty clubs, arrange to go on holiday with a coachload of strangers. But I know I'd be seated next to a woman with broad hips and a perspiration problem or, worse, a man picked to woo me. I have been on one blind date, in the early days after my husband left, before I had more sense.

I answered one of those ads in the paper. Daphne encouraged me. She said, 'What have you got to lose?' and laughed when it went wrong.

My 'Unusual man, owns own business, needs an understanding companion' turned out to be an immigrant from Estonia, with very poor English. He could only talk fluently about his egg farm; a smallholding crammed between a row of council houses and Billingston's Methodist Chapel. Instead of a rose, he handed me a brown bag crammed with bad lays. I flushed the eggs, some no bigger than strawberries, down my toilet.

*

I look at my watch, forty-five minutes to go. I push the food plates around on the cloth till they look appealing. I polish the wine glasses. I dust the tea cups and coffee cups and place them in rows upon the broad mantelpiece. I am disturbed, unsure whether to stay, to welcome people to the funeral tea, or leave. I sit on Daphne's floral sofa, try to reach a decision.

I'd like to avoid the tea. I'm not in the mood to share memories about Daphne, to swap anecdotes. Neither do I want to counter those who'll go on about Daphne's bizarre dress sense, her loud voice and crazy behaviour. But I ought to stay, for Jeff, and because I need to get it into my head that Daphne has really gone.

I kick off my shoes and curl my legs upon the sofa. I move a cushion, to place it behind my back. I look around the room. I haven't closed the doors on the tallboy and can see the small tin box. It glistens, and something comes over me.

I pick up the box and return to the sofa. I run my fingers over the embossed design, feeling the elephants' tusks and trunks tickle my skin. I turn the key and lift the lid.

The box is empty except for a small brown envelope. The envelope is marked '1962' and is unsealed. I can see a wad of photographs crammed inside. I prise the photographs from the envelope.

The photographs are black and white. I haven't seen them before and can't imagine why. Because Daphne was fond of taking pictures and fond of showing the results. I've spent many evenings in Daphne's front room flicking through her albums, laughing at the images. Daphne arranged her albums according to subject. There was the Daphne Album, the Jeff Album, the Daphne and Mickey Album, the Men Before Mickey Album, the Holiday Album, the Daphne and Audrey Album.

The first few photographs are of a seaside town. I recognize the town, but can't put a name to it. It is a seedy place. Litter blows down the promenade. Beach umbrellas lie upon the sand, half unfurled. One photo is of a Jack Russell peeing up a rusted lamppost.

The images have a strange feel. Each one is like seeing something I was once part of. Each one says *déjà vu*. But I can't be certain. I take my time, examining the photographs, turning them this way, holding them upside down, looking for clues, for inspiration. I wonder if they belong to Jeff. I wonder if I should mention them when he returns from the funeral.

I decide not to. Halfway down the pack, people start to appear. A group of women, hunched together, laughing, pointing at the camera. A single shot of a small boy. The boy is Jeff. He's wearing his primary shorts, his sweater with the too-long sleeves. His black hair is plastered to his scalp, shiny with oil. Carefully I place him to the side. And there it is. Daphne and I standing arms linked, smiles wide and happy upon our faces.

My husband took the photograph. I remember now. It was on a day trip to Cromer. And for a while Daphne and I lost Jeff and my husband. I don't know how it happened. It wasn't planned. Neither was the salty kiss. We were just walking along the beach, arm in arm. The wind was cold. There was the sickening smell of fried breakfasts. I turned to Daphne to say something about my sandals letting in the wet, when our bodies seemed to meet. The kiss was long. I could taste the sea on Daphne's lips, feel a desperation in the open mouth, the thick front teeth. 'What is it, Daphne?' I whispered.

She shook her head, pulled away from me. 'Let's find your old man,' she said, switching on her bright, bright smile. 'Get him to take a photo. A nice one of you and me. A buddy shot.'

I wake. It is still night. I've been having my dream again. The same dream I've had since Daphne died. I roll back my duvet, allowing the chilly air to creep across my body. I look at my thickening thighs, run my hands over the rounded shape of my stomach. I never used to be so plump.

I find it strange that my dream hasn't changed. I expected

it to. Because, on waking, my mind is still coloured by the kiss. To this day I do not know what Daphne was asking of me. We never spoke about it, and obviously Daphne wanted to hide it away, not put it in the photograph albums as an official part of her life.

And me? What did I think about the touch?

I remember confusion.

I remember sensing need.

I remember how lovely her teeth felt.

I remember wanting more.

I remember crying and drinking and twice planning to visit Daphne with my bags packed, ready to say, ready to ask.

Till time began to blur. Till the everyday became more persuasive. Till the need became hidden, secreted away.

I turn on my side, check my alarm clock. It is set for eight. The little red hand points conscientiously to the big brown eight. And I laugh. I have no idea why. But suspect it's something to do with embarrassment. And loss. The laugh is loud. Hysterical. Gulping. It cripples me and I curl with the stitch. When the stitch subsides I feel so hot I have to pull off my nightie. Then I comfort myself. I'm clumsy at first. But soon I have the rhythm. I sink into it and try to imagine what it would have been like. If we'd been brave.

Her hair was so black. It flew around my face as we kissed. It was like being touched by magic. It made the world seem beautiful, mysterious. It made my body burn and opened me raw.

Dicky Disaster

Christmas 1993. Visiting time. We've done my relatives. Now, we're at Richard's. His dad's.

We are in the living room. Richard and I sit crushed together on a two-seater velour sofa. The ugliest sofa ever. The type I laugh at in furniture shops.

The sofa is new; it's replaced a cane affair. It matches the wallpaper, which the cane never did. The velour is printed with a similar design. Purple and shiny, with flecks of silver.

I hate visiting family, especially Richard's dad's. We live miles away, which means we drop in only at Christmas, but it's still too often. Because they can't cope with us. You can see it on their faces when they open the front door. First the fake smiles, then the panic.

They're here. They're here. What to do? What to do?

We are left on the doorstep watching them scurry away. His dad into the kitchen. His dad's second wife to the telephone in the bedroom, to make the call she just has to make. Her son to the video in the living room, because he needs to set it, because he doesn't want to miss his favourite programme: that quiz show where the sequinned-suited guy runs down a flight of stairs shouting, 'Questions and answers! Plain and simple!'

As the hall empties before us, Richard tries to laugh it off. Ha! Ha! He throws his head back to issue this dreadful laugh. I thump his arm to shut him up, then drag him over the threshold and into the living room. Every year it's the same.

Now, we sit on the sofa, watching Richard's step-brother twiddle with the video. We don't speak. Richard's step-brother is concentrating. His tongue juts out between his lips, his eyes focus intently on the video's digital display. At one point he farts. A rich wet noise bullets from his backside to greet us. But he doesn't apologize. He doesn't acknowledge the indiscretion. He continues to press buttons, until the posse arrives.

Richard's dad venturing forth, to bring us cups of coffee. 'Here we are,' he says, edging into the living room. A funny shaped man, with stooping shoulders and a pot belly. He is going bald; I can see the soft yellow of his pate as he bends to place the cups on the coffee table.

'One for me?' asks Richard's step-brother. He eases awkwardly into the low armchair beside us.

'On the table.' Richard's dad looks at him. 'Won't be a minute,' he says, scuttling back into the kitchen.

I nudge Richard. It's like his dad is attached to the kitchen by a run of elastic. Just manages to spend thirty seconds in the living room before PING! the elastic returns him to his hidy-hole.

The kitchen with the brown fitted units. The battered stainless steel sink with mixer tap. The beige lino. And Dicky the budgie. The ancient ugly bird which sits in a cage on top of the refrigerator, pecking itself like it has pecked itself day in day out for all of its life.

'How old is Dicky?' I once asked Richard.

'Too old,' Richard replied.

Richard's step-brother looks at the carpet, jabbing his slippers at its geometric pattern. I can tell he's feeling duped. He thought it was safe to move from the video. When Richard's dad came into the room, he thought he could relax, leave it up to him. The small talk. The chit chat. The exchanging of pleasantries.

I clear my throat. I always have to start. 'All set now?' I ask.

'Oh yes,' he says.

'That's good,' I encourage.

'Oh yes,' he says.

'Is it *The Crazy Craig Show*?' I persist.

Though he's a grown man, I feel sorry for him. I ask this question knowing I'm offering him the chance to talk assuredly. Because he loves Crazy Craig. Crazy Craig is his life.

'Of course it's Crazy Craig,' he smiles suddenly. 'The man is a star.' Then, 'He nearly died, you know.'

'No!' I say.

'Yes,' he replies. 'He fell down a manhole. Some prat left the lid off and Crazy Craig slipped in. But he had those reins on. Those baby reins. And they caught on a piece of pipe and stopped him from falling right down. His mum was able to pull him out.'

'His mum?' I ask.

'He was two,' he says.

I stir my coffee, watch the shiny teaspoon cut the thick sluggish liquid. Richard shifts beside me. I can feel him working himself up to speak, to contribute.

'Is Crazy Craig married yet?' he asks.

I smile and bring my coffee cup to my lips to disguise it. I watch Richard's step-brother over the brim of the cup. He's pushing his puffy hands through his hair. His eyes are bright. He opens his mouth and his eager voice fills the garish box-like room.

In one corner of the room, behind the large round table where we will eat our festive dinner, is the Christmas tree. Quite a big tree. A plastic tree decorated with tinsel and fairy lights. It reminds me of the tree my parents used to have. The tree my sister and I would fight to dress. Because we imagined it was a magic tree and that touching it would somehow make our dreams come true. My mother threw the tree on the council tip, the day after father died. 'I never liked the thing,' she explained. 'I prefer real.'

And I prefer real too. Now I'm older. I can't stand glitter, gaudiness. I'm not into sticking Santa heads on my walls, or trailing chains of foil across my ceilings, or spraying fake snow on my windows. Richard's step-mother has sprayed MERRY

XMAS TO OUR NEIGHBOURS on her living-room window.

She sees me looking at her artwork as she enters the room. 'It's good, isn't it?' she says. She's a small woman with tidy hair. She wears a neat jumper with pearly buttons done up to the neck, a pair of unfashionable slacks which are elasticated at the waist and mule slippers. Though she has spent the last half an hour hidden from us, speaking on the phone, she's more at ease in our company than her men. I can't get my head round her.

'Very good,' I reply. I watch as she sits by her son, on the arm of the comfy chair.

He doesn't acknowledge her. He continues to tell the story of Crazy Craig's unhappy romances. She pats him on the back, a slow stroking pat, and she talks over him. 'It took me ages,' she says. 'Because I had to write it backwards. It was very difficult to do.'

'Yes,' I say. 'I can imagine.'

'But then,' she adds, 'I wanted to cheer up the next-door-but-ones. They've had a terrible year. Their grandson was jailed for robbing the post office, then someone put a bomb through their letter box. A fire bomb! It ruined the hall carpet and set their cat alight. Poor thing sleeps in the living room now, curled up on the telephone directories. It had to have an ear removed and it can't see any more. It's totally blind.'

'No, it's not,' says Richard's dad, sticking his head through the open serving hatch in the wall. He holds a can of beer in his hand and he peers across the dining table to address us. 'It can see shapes.'

My first Christmas with Richard was spent in a damp cottage in Mousehole. Pretty Mousehole with its tiny stone harbour. We walked along the harbour wall, smelling the sea as it misted the air. We watched shabby rowing boats rock on the waves. We bought milk in glass bottles from the local store.

It was the loveliest Christmas. A bright sparkly frost coated the pavements. Everything was fresh and we played 'Imagine'.

'Imagine if you were a brain surgeon,' said Richard. 'You could wear a green hat and those sexy rubber gloves.'

'I could up your IQ.'

'You could rummage around.'

'I could make you forget, take away your memory.'

'My sense of guilt.'

We've never had a better Christmas. Because now we're a regular item we have to share ourselves out. We have to give ourselves up on the important occasions. To the people who litter our early photo albums. To the relatives. The ghostly figures who will always haunt us.

I chase my mince pie around the plate. It slides in the cream and my fork cannot still it.

The atmosphere is easier. We've had our Christmas Sunday meal. We've drunk plenty of shorts and beer. We're looser, merrier, less on guard.

Richard's dad has had the most to drink. He even swapped his mince pie for a Greek liqueur. His face has turned a blistering red and he's bombarding us with tragic tales. Tales of disaster and dreadful catastrophe.

He repeated the story about next-door-but-one, then moved on to the burst water mains which flooded the local library and ruined the paperback carousel. Now he's telling us about last week's sniper scare in the city centre. How a ten-year-old boy with a pea shooter sent shoppers into panic. Rat-a-tat-tat! The peas ricocheted against shop shutters, and a family who'd recently had a bad holiday in Belfast went into overdrive. They linked hands and ran through the precinct shouting, 'Get your heads down!'

'Can you believe it?' said Richard's dad. 'A pensioner got crushed in the rush to escape.'

'Poor woman,' added Richard's step-mother. 'They broke her glasses. Her face was covered in blood.'

'Is she dead?' asked Richard.

'Oh yes. Very.'

It is nearly time to leave. Richard's step-brother watches his Crazy Craig video. Richard's step-mother is back on the phone. Richard's dad is slumped across the dining table. Occasionally he looks up to say, 'You still here, son?' or 'How's the do-gooding?'

Richard is a social worker. His dad can't handle this. He mentions Richard's job only when he is drunk, when he has the licence to mock, the freedom to forget.

Richard knows this, and it's sadder than sad. Because Richard loves his job. He helps kids speak out. He listens to them as they struggle with their family secrets, the awful things which their daddy or mummy, grandpa or grandma, brothers or sisters say they must hide away, keep silent about. 'Yes, Papa is bad to me. I didn't fall. I didn't trip. Papa kicked me. He kicked me down the stairs.'

Richard tells his dad about his work. He's nervous. He starts some story about this single parent who lives in a caravan with her three children, two cats, seven guinea pigs and cockatoo. I've heard about this woman, how she clings to her children and her animals, not wanting to give up any of them. Although it's necessary. Although the caravan stinks of piss and pet food, and the children have had worms. It's not a funny story. But Richard is laughing. His hysterical laugh. The dreadful laugh which I only hear when he's with his family.

I begin to tidy the dinner dishes, unable to speak, to make things any easier. I push the dishes through the hatch, then head for the kitchen.

'Hello, Dicky,' I say to the ancient budgerigar, sitting in its cage on top of the refrigerator.

The tatty creature ignores me. It pecks at its belly, plucking the few feathers it has.

I close the hatch, shutting out Richard and his relatives, and take the dishes to place them in the sink. I run the tap to swill the remaining pools of gravy and cream. Then I press my head against the bars of Dicky's cage.

'BOO!' I shout, and the decrepit bird topples from its perch.

Richard and I walk to the train station, to catch the train to his mum's. Because Richard's dad won't have us sleeping over at his place. He has never asked us to. He has never even offered to drive us to the station. He has never put himself out. Though he makes his calls, where he says, 'So you'll be coming home to see us at Christmas, son? Don't forget your dad at Christmas.'

'Well,' I say to Richard. 'Poor Dicky.'

'I know,' he says. 'Poor Dicky.'

I squeeze his hand. I'm not sure if he is upset. He's gone very quiet since I told him how Dicky died, since I told him the truth. Because I wasn't able to be honest at his dad's. I couldn't tell them I'd murdered their pet. I had to pretend I found the bird lying comatose on the bottom of the cage. 'Old age,' I diagnosed. 'We all have to go at some time.'

We stood in the kitchen with our heads bowed while Richard's family swapped Dicky stories. The day Richard's dad brought Dicky home from the pet shop. The day Dicky nibbled his cuttlefish, ate his chickweed, rang the bell which dangles from the roof of his cage. I looked at Richard then, smiled at him, and he smiled back. He was finding it funny, I could tell.

But now I'm not too sure. 'Well, they asked for it,' I say, defensively. 'All they did was talk about disasters. They were willing it to happen. They were dying to have their own personal calamity.'

'They've already got one of them,' says Richard. 'Me.'

I stop. I tug Richard's arm to make him stop too. This is sounding serious. 'No,' I say. 'No, they won't admit to that. Because you're better than them. You've moved on. How can they tell anyone they're disappointed in you? Nobody would understand. But they can go to town on Dicky.'

'Do you think it'll bring us closer together?' asks Richard. 'Something Dad and I can share?'

His face is impenetrable, worrying. I touch his lips and am about to say 'Oh Richard' when he laughs his wonderful laugh. The laugh which I know and love. Our laugh.

'Give us a kiss,' he says.

Marbles

The Southside Methodist seems miles away to you. Mr Brown drives you there in his long thin car. You love his car: its creamy paintwork, its leather upholstery, the shiny burgeoning bumpers. You curl on the back seat, so nobody can see you, with Mr Brown's travel blanket pulled up to your chin: the blanket blue and green, warm and plush against your skin.

'Well,' says Mr Brown as he drives steadily, efficiently. 'How are you today?'

'Fine,' you reply.

'And your marbles?' he asks.

'They're fine too,' you say.

You are a small child, ten years old. You live with your grandparents in a two-up, two-down. A terraced house with no back garden and no front yard, which opens on to a filthy street.

You spend most of your time on the street, because your grandparents don't want you indoors. Your grandfather dislikes children (especially you) and your grandmother doesn't want to upset him. Besides, she is houseproud and you fingermark the furniture. She gave you the marbles. 'To use outside,' she said.

You didn't say thanks. You held the marbles in your hands, jiggled their hard round bodies. You lined them along the kerb, willing them to move, to do something. You would've dropped them down the drain except for Mr Brown.

Mr Brown is an imposing man. He is tall, wears suits and has a la-di-da voice. He is not well liked round the neighbourhood. Your grandparents curse him. They also let him into their house every Friday and give him money which he puts inside a slim red notebook.

'Mind you don't trip, Brown,' called your grandfather one collecting day. 'Mind you don't go and break your neck.'

'Sorry?' said Mr Brown, stepping around you and your trail of danger. He picked up a straggler and handed it back to you, and the following Friday he showed you how to toss and spin and jump the marbles.

Mr Brown stops the car. 'Cheeseburger or plain?' he asks.

'Cheese,' you reply.

You sit up. You have passed from the north of the city to the south. You have travelled through the Cally Tunnel under the river which separates the two halves of the city. Mr Brown doesn't like the tunnel because it's always jammed with traffic. But you like it. It is tiled with a shimmering turquoise glass, like thousands of broken marbles mosaicked together, and it has its own special sound. A shoosh, shoosh, shoosh.

The sound reminds you of the busy fan heater your mother used to warm her bathroom with, the tiny bathroom with the deep chipped tub.

A petrol station and roadside café mark the end of the Cally Tunnel and the entrance to the south. If there's time Mr Brown tops up his petrol and buys you something for lunch. He used to buy you a hot dog until you said sausages hurt your stomach. Now you get to choose your own burger and eat it as Mr Brown drives down leafy lanes to the Methodist.

You lift the lid of the burger and poke at the square of barely melted cheese. You look out the window. Everything is different here. The houses are large, the roads are prettier. There are more trees. The people are smarter too: they wear nicer clothes. Mr Brown has never said, but you imagine he must live in the south.

Drizzle begins to pitter against the windscreen. Mr Brown switches on the wipers. They make a soft whooshing noise as he turns into the alleyway.

132

The alleyway lies between a children's play area and a residential home for the elderly. It is as wide as Mr Brown's car and enclosed by hedges and a thick canopy of foliage. It reminds you of the Cally Tunnel, except it is darker and quieter and more private. You always visit the alleyway before going to the Methodist.

You cram the last of your burger in your mouth, then open the travel bag placed behind the driver's seat. You pull out the clothing: the woollen smock, the white tights, the neat shoes, the Aran cardigan with its large leather buttons. You take off your tracksuit and put on the fancy dress.

Mr Brown ignores you while you change. He busies himself, running a washcloth over the car's dashboard, wiping it around the steering wheel. You are glad he doesn't look at you, because you feel exposed undressing and dressing, your narrow chest flashing pink and young as you drop the smock over your head.

'Ready now?' asks Mr Brown eventually.

'Yes,' you say.

Mr Brown turns to face you, smiles at the transformation. Then says, 'Right, let's see.'

You take a clutch of marbles from your tracksuit pockets. You hold them high, before tucking them into the pocket of the Aran. Mr Brown's concession. He has told you your marbles belong to your other life, there is no place for them here, but that he'll allow you to take a handful to the Methodist. To touch. For comfort.

You are not grateful.

Having the toys only worries you. You're afraid they may make a noise; or, worse, drop from the pocket. You see them as mini bombs waiting to blow. But you can't tell Mr Brown this. Because he wouldn't appreciate it, his kindness being spurned.

Mr Brown puts his key in the ignition. 'Don't forget to tidy your hair,' he says, before starting the engine.

You nod. You bend to bundle your tracksuit into the bag,

133

then fish out the comb. You drag it through your hair as Mr Brown drives to the Methodist.

The Southside Methodist is a modest red stone building, with no steeple, or spire. It sits awkwardly beside a row of elegant three-storey homes. It resembles a hostel and inside it is just as austere, except for the embroidered cloth which covers the altar and the statue of Jesus.

The statue was carved by a local resident who works as a dentist during the day and practises sculpture at night. The statue is wooden and painted. It is as colourful as a fairground stall. Jesus's skin is a shrimp pink, the blood from his bright green crown of thorns is crimson. He wears a startling white cloth over his privates. His eyes are an icy blue and they remind you of your largest marble.

The drizzle falls on the porch covering the entrance to the Methodist. Mr Brown lets down his umbrella and shakes it. He stands it in the corner of the porch before easing open the hefty wooden door. It makes a shushing noise like a hard broom pushed over a yard. Your heart beats fast as you follow Mr Brown inside. The smell of the chapel, the good clean smell and the quiet always excite you, make your head feel light, your limbs weightless.

'Ah, Mr Brown,' says Preacher Southam, moving along the red stone floor like a silent Hoover.

You have never seen under the Preacher's cassock, but you imagine he is motorized. You smile at him, feeling shy.

'And your little niece, Betty,' says Preacher Southam, placing an arm around your shoulders. He ushers you into the main body of the chapel.

When Mr Brown first called you his niece you asked him to explain. You knew about your family. You knew you only had a grandmother and a grandfather, no cousins, no aunts or uncles. You knew about your dead mother, and the fly-by-

134

night father who'd planted his seed before disappearing on the train to London. You knew you couldn't be Mr Brown's niece, though you wanted it so very much.

Mr Brown laid your marbles on the ground. He improvised your family tree, drew imaginary lines from marble to marble to indicate relationships. He said it looked a sad little tree, said you needed more relatives to keep you warm, to make you feel secure. 'That's why I've decided to adopt you, to make you my niece,' he said. 'I hope you don't mind. Every girl needs a special uncle, don't you agree?'

'Can you do that?' you said. 'Can you just adopt?'

The chapel is calm. Organ music pipes softly. The music seems to have no source. It floats in the air like a ghostly spirit. You look at Preacher Southam. 'It's lovely here,' you whisper.

Preacher Southam hands you a hymn book, then gently directs you to a pew. The pew is towards the front of the chapel, facing the pulpit and the statue of Jesus. 'Thank you,' you say. You edge along the hard oak seat until you reach the whitewashed chapel wall. You settle yourself against the wall, pulling your dress straight and crossing your legs. You remove your tissues from the sleeves of your Aran and lay them on top of the marbles, pressing them down to prevent their clacking, to stop them from falling out.

'Sshh,' says an old woman from the pew in front. She turns to look at you. Her hair is grey and set tight. Small lacquered rolls perch on her crown like frosted sausages.

'Hello Mrs Vernon,' you say.

'Ah,' says the woman. 'Hello.' Mrs Vernon is a congregation regular. You met her on your first visit to the Southside Methodist.

Mr Brown was very nervous that day. He ran his fingers along the length of his tie. He slid his slim red notebook in and out of his jacket pocket. He tapped the palms of his hands on the car's dashboard. 'Betty,' he said. 'This is a secret. Between you and me.'

You nodded, though you couldn't understand his concern. 'No one will care,' you wanted to say.

But still he doesn't want your friendship to be known. You have to pretend you're his niece when in the south side. When in the north you have to pretend you've no connection, you have to pretend you are strangers. This doesn't bother you. You think it fun.

When he wants to see you he drives down your street and signals from his car. A slight dip of his head, which makes your heart fizz. You watch him journey round the corner into Dugness Drive. Then you gather your marbles, placing them in your tracksuit pockets. You move slowly like he has told you to, counting to one hundred and breathing deeply before skipping to meet him.

He sits with his car engine purring and the back door open. He never greets you, never smiles at you as you clamber in to lie flat on the leather seat. He behaves as if you're invisible, reaching across you to close the door and drop the lock.

'Mrs Vernon,' says Mr Brown as he sits beside you.

'Mr Brown,' says the woman, acknowledging him with a stiff bow of her head. She glances once more at you, before turning to face the pulpit.

The pulpit is wooden and box-shaped. Preacher Southam enters it from the left, climbing three worn stairs to stand on the raised platform. The pulpit suits Preacher Southam. It is the right size, the right height. It embraces him and seems to lift him closer to the heavens, confirms him in his vocation. Unlike the cleric who stood in for Preacher Southam when he went down with suspected appendicitis. This man was squat. He teetered on tiptoes to read the Good Book. He made you snigger.

Preacher Southam opens the chapel Bible, smooths its pages, begins the service. Today's service is subdued, about how life seems so unbearable and God so removed. You listen to Preacher Southam reading Psalm 90 and clutch your hymn book as his familiar voice intones: 'Thou dost sweep men away; they are like a dream.'

You don't understand the service, but notice Mrs Vernon nodding her head. A heaviness coats the sparse congregation, and a young woman runs for the chapel door, blowing her nose loudly as she scurries down the aisle.

You know the woman. Mr Brown linked arms with her at the harvest festival. Everyone was singing about wheat and barley, vegetables and fruits – 'All good gifts around us' – and you and the woman were smiling at Mr Brown, happy. But Mr Brown never told you who the woman was, or why he spoke harshly to her after the festival.

The woman struggles with the hefty chapel door. She tugs it open and a gust of rainy wind strikes her, lifting her hair so she looks spooked. Mr Brown puts his hand under your chin, turns your face from the unsavoury sight.

'Let us pray,' says Preacher Southam as the woman pulls the door shut, leaving a sprinkling of water on the threshold and a yellowing leaf.

You unhook your hassock and kneel beside Mr Brown. His head is bowed. His hands hang limp against his thighs. You shadow him. You mumble when he mumbles, sigh when he sighs, say Amen and look heavenward at the end of prayers for suffering children.

Heavenward is the Methodist ceiling, whitewashed like the surrounding walls, smooth and uninteresting except for a fissure which runs above the statue of Jesus. A steady drip of rain squeezes through the crack to land on his bright green crown of thorns, to cross his forehead like a wayward tear. You will tell Mr Brown about this, to impress him: you know he wants his special girl to be observant, bright and clever.

He always checks you over before you enter the Methodist. He signs at you to straighten your cardigan, brush the creases from your dress, flatten your hair. 'Now remember,' he says. 'You are my niece. Be polite. Be good. Do me justice.'

Mr Brown can be cruel if you don't behave well. The first time he punished you was after you'd sniggered at the cleric. Mr Brown was nice as nice until you reached his car. Then he made you bend over the back seat. He pulled down your pants and hit you. He belted your bottom, your thighs, your calves, hit them hard with his big wide hands. 'I don't like naughty girls,' he said. 'I'm a proud man. I have a reputation. I don't want it spoilt.'

You cried. You said, 'Sorry. Sorry. Sorry.' Over and over you apologized. But Mr Brown said it was too late for apologies and continued to hit you. When finally he stopped, you vowed never to see him again.

You ignored his car when he drove it along your street. You ignored his secret signal. You made sure you weren't about when he visited your grandparents' house on Friday evenings. You kept your distance for three weeks. Until you couldn't stand the boredom. Until you couldn't bear the emptiness, the unfriendliness, the cold chill which blew around you as you flicked and rolled your marbles.

He's slapped you since and he's punched you in the stomach. But you're learning. You are learning to be the niece he wants. Though it is difficult. It is the most difficult thing you have ever had to do and sometimes it gives you a headache, sometimes it makes you worry. Because anything can upset him. Any little thing.

One night, when you were especially worried, you drew a stick picture of your grandparents and a stick picture of Mr Brown. You put the pictures on the floor and considered them. You thought about what they gave you, what they took from you, how they made you feel. You placed a marble beneath the pictures when you thought of something good about them, subtracted a marble when you thought of something bad. When your thinking was done six marbles trailed from the feet of your grandparents, thirteen from Mr Brown.

Because most days you feel happy, feel you love Mr Brown, wouldn't want to be without him. You imagine outings. You dream of getting in his car and being driven to the seaside, eating a picnic and having fun. Your dreams are in Technicolor, every detail pronounced and significant. Before you met him, you had never considered the future.

The organist begins to play 'Through the night of doubt and sorrow onward goes the pilgrim band'. Preacher Southam signals for the congregation to rise. Mr Brown pushes a broad hand under your elbow to lever you up.

'Oh,' you cry. You stumble as you stand, and a marble spills from your Aran. You watch it hit the stone floor. More marbles follow, scattering loudly. You fumble along the base of your cardigan pocket, find a hole, stop another marble slipping through.

Preacher Southam coughs. He hushes the organist. 'We have had our share of interruptions today.' He smiles. 'Better pick up your toys, Betty, before the twins swallow them, then we'll continue. If you can help your niece, Mr Brown.'

Mr Brown nods. 'Certainly,' he says. His voice is taut. He places a hand on your head, pushes you to the floor.

You begin a frantic search, while Mr Brown gathers up one of the Michael twins. He returns the wobbly toddler to the pew opposite, popping a marble from her mouth. Then he does the same to her brother, placing the chubby boy on his mother's lap.

'We need safety gates on these pews,' says the young woman. She smiles a hopeless weary smile and Mr Brown ignores her.

He drops the marbles he has collected at your feet, then kneels on the floor beside you. He is silent, watching you as you scrabble after your play things. You have most of them in your hand and are reaching for the last which sits beneath a hanging hassock.

Your fingers trap the glass ball, and Mr Brown's fingers follow. He nips your skin, and you stiffen.

*

139

The drizzle ceases and a real rain starts to fall. A thick grey rain which looks solid, which hits the earth with relentless slaps. You watch it batter the car windows. 'I expect the tunnel will be busy,' says Mr Brown. 'Because they won't run the ferry. Not in this weather.' He looks at you in the mirror.

You see him, then nod, then try to smile. 'You're not forgiven yet,' says Mr Brown. He grates his gears from third to second and you bow your head.

You shift on the cold leather of the back seat. This time he used his shoe. Smacking the wide inflexible sole against your flesh. It was worse than his hand, no gaps between fingers to ease the pressure. Just a solid shape hitting and hitting and hitting. And you know he only stopped because some children playing in the ground next to the alleyway were getting curious. Pushing through the thick hedge, trying to find where the noise was coming from.

'Pull your pants up,' he said. His voice was deep and angry. His face blotchy. He reminded you of your grandfather on the day you'd broken the TV.

'I'll fucking kill you,' your grandfather had screamed. 'I'll fucking strangle you.' Then later, when he'd entered your bedroom, 'Why don't you just run away?' he'd whispered. 'Why don't you just leave us be?'

The car edges into the tunnel. Mr Brown switches off the windscreen wipers. You hear the engine's purr, listen to it mingle with the special tunnel sound. The shoosh, shoosh, shoosh.

You had thought about running away. You'd thought about travelling down to London to try to find your father. But the next day Mr Brown had shown you how to play with your marbles, and you'd unpacked your carrier bag, decided to stay.

Now you don't know what to do. You try to imagine what Preacher Southam would suggest, what Jesus would say. But you can only see pictures. Preacher Southam moving silent around the still harsh chapel, mouthing invisible words. And

Jesus, garish and dying, dumb with his sad and solitary tear.

The traffic slows. Mr Brown puts the car into first. An orange bus sits in front. Grey smoke puffs from its exhaust. On its boot is an advert for an indigestion remedy: a smiling woman holds a green lozenge and says, 'What a relief I remembered Relief'.

You shift in your seat again and your marbles clack, a tiny sound, but not tiny enough. Not tiny enough to escape Mr Brown. He turns round. 'Did I hear right?' he says. 'Did I hear those marbles?'

You look at him, there is nothing you can say. You wanted to throw your marbles away, but Mr Brown wouldn't let you. He stuffed them into your tracksuit pockets after you'd changed from the smock, told you the marbles weren't the problem, you were.

Mr Brown pulls on the handbrake, puts the car into neutral. He leans over his seat to release the lock on the door closest to you. He reaches for the door handle and pushes the door open. 'Out,' he orders. 'Walk home.'

You look at Mr Brown and start to cry.

'Go on,' he says. His face is pinched, tight. His stare forces you to dangle your legs outside the car. You're not wearing socks and a sudden waft of heat bites the exposed skin of your ankles. A horn beeps. The traffic stirs in the lane opposite and Mr Brown tuts.

'You've missed your chance,' he says. He releases his handbrake and begins to move off. 'Close the door,' he says.

And you jump.

It is only a small jump, an impulsive jump. It is only a small jump, but you feel like you are flying as you let go of the chilly leather upholstery, as you launch into the heady air.

You have one clear memory of your mother. You are about four or five. It is bathtime. Your mother has stripped off your clothes, has lifted you into the deep chipped tub. The water is shallow and tepid and your mother helps you to sit in it. Then she removes the cap from a Matey bubble bath and squeezes the plastic tube in the shape of a sailor. You move your hands in the water, making bubbles from the blue Matey liquid. The bubbles rise.

'Are you having fun?' asks your mother. 'Is this fun?' Your mother has a round face, her eyes are small. Her hair has no real colour. She's wearing a pink sweater with a zip-up neck.

You shiver, and your mother says, 'But it's supposed to be summer.' Then she switches on the fan heater. A cosy sound fills the bathroom. It is soothing. It is warm like a warm heart.

You want to tell your mother how much you like it, but she is wiping her face on a towel. And so you don't tell her, because you know what she's doing. She's trying to muffle her tears. She's trying to hide her sorrow, her ever-present sorrow.

You hit the dirty concrete road which runs through the Cally Tunnel. You fall flat and bang your head on the hard surface. You feel a jolt of pain as it travels from the back of your head to the front. And you are in darkness.

A strange darkness full of strange sounds. Indistinct sounds. Watery sounds. Otherworldly sounds. Now and then you hear car horns toot, you hear voices. Different voices saying different things.

    – She all right?
    – An ambulance!
    – How?
    – Broken child lock?
    – Niece? Your niece?
    – Pretty.
    – Isn't she.

A strange darkness full of strange smells. Thick cloying smells which push their way up your nostrils, which seem to puff behind your eyes.

But you are not frightened. You are calm. Your body seems centred and still, and you wonder if you are dead. You wonder if this is what it is like to be dead.

And as you wonder the darkness fades, pales to a grey and then to a white, and then you see yourself, reflected in the curved shimmering ceiling of the Cally Tunnel. You look beautiful, like an artist has painted you, a real artist. Split open marbles decorate your hair. One a bright red. One a bright orange. One a yellow like the yellow of a happy happy sun. Twinkling and free.

You lie on the back seat of Mr Brown's car, with Mr Brown's travel blanket pulled up to your chin: the blanket blue and green, warm and plush against your skin.

You have a headache. A terrible headache which makes you want to moan. But you don't. You keep quiet. Because Mr Brown is quiet. Because his very tenseness and stillness tells you that you should be quiet.

He lifted you into his car. He laid you on the seat. He tucked the blanket around you and thanked everyone who had stopped to help; told them all he would be taking you to hospital, for a check-up, because head injuries are risky, dangerous.

He thanked everyone, as he took your hands from under the blanket and filled them with your broken marbles.

'My niece's toys,' he explained. 'She wouldn't want to leave them behind.'

And now he drives the car from the Cally Tunnel into the north of the city. You cannot see the small terraced houses, the narrow streets and the litter blowing along the pavements. But you can feel it. You can sense the gloominess, the grey which discolours the air.

You move a little, trying to curl from the dinginess and you wonder if Mr Brown will take you to the hospital or whether he will drop you off at your grandparents' or leave you on Dugness Drive though you can't really walk.

You move a little, and the broken marbles drop from your

hands. You hear them faintly. The shards patter to hit the travel bag nestled on the floor. A sound like nails falling on rubber. An irritating sound. A sound bound to annoy.

You tense and wait for Mr Brown's reaction. A fluttering feeling rising in your stomach. You close your eyes. Your head swirls with a sharp and nasty pain, and you wait.

You don't like the wait.

And then you feel the car slow and you release a tiny breath.

They found your mother lying in an alleyway. She'd been drinking, the policewoman said, and had taken pills.

They found her lying, curled like a child curls in its bed; her knees tucked against her chest, her hands clutching her cold bare calves. Her face had been washed by the night's rain. Her mascara, blusher, foundation washed away to reveal a young woman, too young. A pathetic sight.

The policewoman told your grandparents she was sorry, and wished she didn't have to be the bearer of such bad news.

'It's all right,' said your grandfather. 'She never was much good.'

Sleep

If you're going to give birth, eject the baby at a reasonable hour. About 8.00 p.m. Have an early evening birth and sleep will be a doddle.

Baby was born at lunchtime, seven months ago. Baby was a ventouse suction baby. After twenty hours the obstetrician fitted a rubber cap on baby's head and tugged and pulled her out of me.

Baby was born at lunchtime. She was hungry. She screamed while the nurses weighed her and cleaned her and wrapped little plastic tags around her skinny red wrists. 'Not a timid one,' they said, as they laid her on my chest.

Baby couldn't find a nipple and tall nurse had to help her. Tall nurse pinched my teat and ran it around baby's mouth. Tall nurse wasn't gentle. She wasn't in the mood; my sick was down her apron, my blood on her pumps.

Baby drank as they wheeled us to maternity. Baby drank as they lifted us on to the high hard bed. Baby drank as the pain pinched through my numbness.

Baby drank and then fell asleep. A long long sleep.

Sleep.

I love sleep. I've always grabbed my full whack, going to bed early and getting up late. Once my head hits the pillow, that's me. Off to Nod.

My mother would try to part us. She'd crouch at the side of my bed when we were in a clinch. She'd blow on my closed eyes and would whisper, 'Wakey wakey, Janey. Don't let the world slip by.'

My mother was an insomniac. Sleep was cruel and treated

her bad. It would flee from her at night, then kiss her briefly as she cooked the tea. I'd find her prone amongst the vegetable peelings, snuffling and snoring anxious snores.

I wasn't the kindest daughter. I was a tease. 'Mum,' I'd say, 'give me sleep over sex, sleep over parties, sleep over a good meal. I prefer sleep to men, to money, to love, to admiration, adoration. Sleep is better than work, better than TV, magazines, videos, dancing, aerobics, shopping and cuddly toys.'

Sleep is.

Sleep is no longer.

My lack of it is coming between us – my man, my baby and me.

It is 2.00 a.m. My man is in bed. He is zonked. It is 2.00 a.m. and I'm in the living room. The lights are dimmed. The gas fire on. It flickers warm orange flickers across the walls, the rug, the baby buggy. Baby is in the buggy. She's smiling at me. Occasionally she lifts her hands to catch the fire flickers.

Baby is happy. She's forever happy at 2.00 a.m. Our nighttime is her daytime. I sit in the fireside chair watching her, pushing the buggy backwards, forwards with my feet.

We have a rota now, my man and me. One night on. One night off. One night rocking baby. One night sleeping.

We had no such rota when she was drinking from me. I was the only one who could pacify. Baby clung to my breasts like the neediest leech.

It was easier then. I lived according to her rules. She would suck from me when she wanted. Little sips while the sky was black; little sips between playing and laughing. Sleepy, greedy gulps in the morning.

She would conk out at noon. My man would come home for lunch to find us in bed. But he didn't complain. He barely said a word. Our lives weren't synchronized enough for chat.

*

146

Who told us we should change our ways? Who said 'Baby should be put on the bottle and made to sleep at night?'

The midwives. The health visitor. Our bank account.

I had to go back to work.

I work in a chemist's. I help behind the pharmacy counter. I wear a blue overall and a charming smile. I commiserate with people who complain about the price of prescriptions. I listen to stories of minor and major sufferings: verrucas, ear wax, sprained ankles, blocked arteries, broken arms, terminal cancer, osteoporosis. I give out bandages, incontinence pads and neck braces, powders and lotions, creams and pills.

I am an angel of helpfulness and sympathy.

Or I was.

I returned to work four months ago. Baby went to the childminder's.

The childminder enthuses over baby. 'This kid is no trouble, no trouble at all. She's my little drowsy one. She sleeps away the day.'

She sleeps and I slump behind the counter.

Theories.

Theories from baby manuals, old wives and breakfast telly.

WAYS TO GET BABY TO SLEEP AT NIGHT:

1. Keep her awake during the day. Stimulate her! Bounce her and jiggle her. Lay her on a rug of psychedelic shag. Coo at her, laugh with her, sing songs, bombard her with whistles, screeches, fluffy toys, rattles, cotton reels threaded on an old shoe lace.

Good idea. But . . . Childminder only paid £1.50 an hour. Too embarrassed to ask her to do more than watch.

2. Lay baby to sleep in a cradle that rocks. Ah that wavy motion! Baby will think she's back inside the womb, floating in her dreamy world of languid liquid.

Tried it. With a tape of whale music playing soothingly in the background. Baby isn't convinced.

3. Put baby in a separate room to sleep at night. Leave her to cry. Leave her to holler. Leave her to scream dog's abuse. She'll catch on in the end. Mummy and daddy have their needs too – a little how's your father, then sleep in a snoozy lover's knot.

Done it. Couldn't hack it. Baby's cry tweaked our hearts. It sounded angry. It sounded like she'd get her revenge. When she was old enough.

4. Sleep three to a bed. Baby will be comforted. Baby will feel secure. Baby's snores will coincide with yours. Eskimos, Indians and Bushmen do it. It's fun. It makes sense. Babies like a cuddle.

Doing it now. But . . . Baby's playful. She's a wriggler. She presses her heels in our backs, taps our shoulders with her chubby hands. She laughs and blows bubbles and farts major farts. She's too awake. So most nights we give up. One of us takes baby into the living room, to push her in her buggy.

It is 3.00 a.m. and I'm still at it.

I'm standing, pushing the buggy from behind. Baby twists to face me. She's a strong girl now. She can kick and punch. She is assertive. 'Oi! Oi!' she shouts.

'Oi! Oi! To you!' I return.

Baby laughs. She has a lovely laugh, a charming laugh. But I mustn't encourage it. Baby must learn that night is for sleeping. Baby must learn to fit in with the world.

I stare at her with my weary eyes. 'Sshh!' I say. 'Baby go bye-byes.'

My man reads to me from the newspaper every morning. He reads to me whilst I spoon-feed baby with mashed banana, apple purée and caramel custard.

It's our most constant routine. And we savour it.

I glance from baby to my man as he reads and I get a lovely warm feeling. I see a future when everything goes smoothly, when we sleep in unison, play in unison, enjoy one another.

My man has a beautiful voice. He has ambitions to be a disc jockey. At the moment he is a ranger for Parks and Cemeteries.

He wooed me with his voice. It was in the summer. I lay drowsing on the green lawns of Knightswood Park and he drove by in his orange works van. 'Give us a shag,' he shouted.

I sat upright. His voice was like a lullaby, a cooed serenade, a perfectly pitched soothing tune. 'Marry me,' I mouthed.

'Give us a shag first,' he replied.

Two years ago. Light years ago. And now all that's left of that lovey-dovey age is his voice. The soft silky tones which read from the newspaper, which wind around me and caress me and give me hope.

He selects the stories he knows I'll prefer. Not the political stuff, the stories of wars and arms deals, health service cuts and business enterprise zones. But the more personal tales, the domestic day-to-day.

This morning he read about a woman who bundled her four-month-old into a plastic carrier before dropping her in a dustbin. The baby had been crying. It had been crying since birth. It had cried during breakfast, lunch and tea. It had slept fitfully, taking only catnaps and whimpering during those. The woman was exhausted. She wasn't thinking rationally. She wanted rid of her flesh and blood. She wanted peace and she wanted rest.

Her child didn't die. A neighbour found it. The woman was sentenced to five years in prison and her baby was placed in care. The judge said the woman was intelligent, cold and calculating, and had no feelings for her own.

'I'll bet the judge has no kids,' said my man.

And we looked at each other, and then I said, 'I wish you hadn't told me about your van.'

I couldn't understand it, why my man wasn't feeling as tired as me. I would marvel at his fresh-as-a-daisy face, the lack of dark rings under his eyes, his jaunty casual step. 'Are you on something?' I'd ask.

And then he confessed. His workmates are covering for him, doing his shift whilst he kips in the back of his orange works van. They've even bought him some cushions and a couple of blankets from the Army and Navy Stores. Young men. New men. They feel sorry for him.

It is 4.00 a.m. I hold baby to my chest, singing to her as I make up her formula. I am in the kitchen, leaning against the cooker. My body feels stiff. My knees ache. My head aches.

I've reached the desperate hour. The hour when I start to drift, when my eyelids begin to close over my eyes and a fuzzy white noise buzzes in my ears.

The dangerous hour.

The hour when I consider crushing up sedatives pinched from my work, mixing the drug into baby's formula.

To send her into the deepest sleep, the longest sleep.

And when will she wake up? Do I imagine she will wake up? Do I want her to wake up?

It is 4.30 a.m. I stand by our bedroom door with baby in my arms. Baby is drinking her milk. She's drinking her formula milk and kicking her legs.

'Baby,' I say. 'You're killing me.'

I rest my head on the door, listen to my man's snores. Comfortable, rested, fat round snores. Suddenly I hate him and want to abuse him. I want to pull off the bedclothes and kick him in the balls. I want to leave baby with him and run out of the flat, take a train to Stranraer and a ferry to Ireland.

Escape.

I want escape.

Because he's not being fair. He has his orange works van

and his sympathetic mates. He lies down on furry blankets and foam-filled cushions. He's been promised a hot water bottle and cotton pyjamas. He has hours of extra sleep a day. He recharges his batteries. And he doesn't feel guilty.

'It's the luck of the draw,' he told me in his coo coo voice.

My mother's face was haunted by the sleep she never had. Huge panda rings round her eyes. A twitch in her nose. Sallow sunken cheeks. She lived her life in a twilight world. Her head was foggy. Her heart was bitter.

My father was a night watchman. He courted my mother because she was the only woman who could stay awake with him through the darkest hours. But he couldn't bring himself to marry her. Not even when she fell with me.

My mother and father died last year. Together. She went to visit him in his pebble-dash bungalow to argue over old times. His gas heater exploded and the fire and smoke killed them where they sat. At opposite ends of the living room; Mum on the sofa, Dad on my inheritance – the sixties' bean-bag he'd lifted from a skip.

My doctor sent me to a therapist. He was worried the shock might make me miscarry. I talked during the first meeting and the therapist nodded. The following session he let me doze on his couch. 'You're more stable than the monarchy,' he said. 'All you need is rest.'

Sleep on the sick. I could do with it now. But nobody wants to know.

'It's the way it is,' the health visitor says. 'Young children are an endurance test. You should count your blessings. Your child isn't disabled, you're not an elderly primigravida or a single parent, your flat is on the ground floor and has double-glazing.'

I slept most of the week before baby was born. I lay with my huge hard belly weighted to the bed. I slept through heartburn, practise contractions, baby moving and shifting, a pinched nerve in my hip. My sleep was deep, my breathing so shallow my man began to worry.

It was the longest sleep, but it wasn't refreshing. It was hungry and desperate and as black as black.

I woke when my waters broke. I woke to find my man lying beside me: his chest naked and thin, the silk of his boxers lying soft over his stiff short prick.

It is 5.00 a.m. I stand looking out the kitchen window, having lifted the blind to eye the moon. I'm calmer now, more resigned. I'm waiting for 6.00. Baby will slumber then. She's been doing that lately. Getting in a couple of hours before breakfast.

My man is encouraged by this. He thinks the battle is almost over. But then he's getting his z's and his life is sunnier.

The moon is full and mellow yellow. I turn baby to the window and show it her. I say, 'Look, look there's Mr Moon.'

Baby waves her bottle, before letting it drop. It hits the floor. 'Just be nice,' I warn. I go to tap my finger on her chest, a little poke to let her know who's boss. When I notice she has nodded off.

Baby has nodded off.

Her face has fallen into repose. Her eyelids are shut. Her nose moves slowly, in and out like a tiny rodent's. Her mouth blows ooos of drowsiness. I stare at her. She is fetching. I feel delirious. It makes me want to cry.

'Aren't you a good girl?' I whisper to baby, pressing her closer to my body as I turn from the moon and the stars and the purple sky.

It is just past 5.00 a.m. I carry baby into our bedroom, place her in the middle of our bed. She moves a fraction, pressing down into her nappy, flopping her arms outwards. She dreams of suckling, her mouth puckers and slurps. I snuggle up beside her and tuck the quilt around us.

Baby's night-light is on. It glows a reassuring glow from the far side of the bed. Where my man sleeps. I can see him bathed in the soft misty light. His face is relaxed, his skin free of lines and wrinkles, his lips an idle pale pink.

I push my head into my pillows, try to make use of the extra hour baby has given me. A lovely present. A joyous present. The best.

But I cannot fall. My man is whistling. A low happy snoozy whistle. It is annoying. It makes me want to shake him, to shut him up, to wake him, so I can tell him how his life is cushier than mine.

I do it.

'Ugh,' he grunts. But he doesn't wake.

I do it again.

'Ugh,' he grunts. He pulls himself to the edge of the bed, away from baby, away from me.

'Jim,' I say. 'You're such a fucker.'

He doesn't respond. He clutches the quilt under his chin. His eyes shift beneath his lids. He is dreaming. A golden dream, I know. Because I can sense it. I can see it. The green fields. The daisies. Me in a flowery summer frock, with baby balanced on my hip. Beautiful baby dressed in white, her blond hair glistening in the light.

I decide to give him ten more minutes. Wait until he's reached the finale, the cosy end of the reel. Then I'll go for it. I'll knock him from his privileged perch.

I reach for the alarm clock and turn it to face me. I watch the luminous second hand tick around the dial.

I'm such a clock-watcher now. Like my mum. Like my dad. The hands on the clock are so important to me; how they move, when they move, what's happening while they move.

When I'm at work I stand watching the clock, ignoring the sick as they edge their prescriptions along the counter. I mark the minutes and twist inside as I imagine baby asleep at her childminder's, my man snoozing in the back of his orange works van.

I'm trying not to be obsessive. I'm trying to be mature. I want to believe it won't be for long. This hazy, messy, torturous time. But it's difficult, more than difficult.

I watch the luminous second hand, but the bed is so cosy and warm. It is ripe with the heavy rich smell of my man and the sweet talcum-powder whiff of baby. It is gorgeous. It is getting to me. Thick puffy pillows nestle my head. Tick, tick, tick lulls the clock.

The best thing about sleep is that moment before you drop. That luxurious thick feeling which fills your insides, and the deepening dark which rises between your eyelids and eyes, which seeps through your head.

I try to fight it.
Honestly I try.
But fighting my one true love is not my forte.
Fighting is not my forte.
Sleep is . . .